THE SARAH DOGWOOD STORY

The Sarah Dogwood Story
A Lucas Penny Book
Book 2
By Jared McVay

Published by Creative Texts Publishers, LLC
PO Box 50
Barto, PA 19504
www.creativetexts.com

ISBN: 978-1-64738-060-1

THE SARAH DOGWOOD STORY

A LUCAS PENNY BOOK

BOOK 2

by

Jared McVay

"Where the unknown exists

man is destined to seek out

even if it is by accident"

Table of Contents

ONE

Lucas Penny opened his eyes just enough to look at his surroundings. His head ached and his eyes felt like someone was sticking hot pokers in them.

He was lying on a cot attached to the wall and a short distance away, he could see steel bars from the floor to the ceiling.

With all his effort, he swung his legs over the side of the bed and sat up – immediately regretting his decision. His stomach was doing flip-flops and he felt like he was going to puke.

Lucas took a deep breath to help with the whirling that was going on in his head. He reached up and felt the lumps and dried blood stuck in his hair. With further inspection, Lucas realized his hair hung down to his shoulders and he had a full, raggedy beard that also had blood matted in it.

He stood up and put his hand against the wall to hold himself steady until he could gain his balance.

Once the whirling in his head went away, he looked at himself and found his clothes were not only filthy, but torn and also laced with blood spots. Upon further inspection, he realized he was inside a jail cell and on the far side of the cell, he saw a black man sitting on a bunk just like the one he had been on. He too, looked like he'd been in a fight and Lucas wondered if it had been the two of them that had tangled?

The man grinned and said, "Welcome back to the world of the living. Feeling pretty rough, I'm guessing."

When Lucas tried to speak, he felt pain in his jaw. "Where am I and why am I in jail?"

The man shook his head and said, "Whooie, either you tied one on something fierce, or else all those blows you took to your head did something to your memory."

Lucas tried to remember where he was and the reason he was in jail, but nothing came to mind. He slumped back down on his cot and put his hands to his aching head. "I can't remember anything at the moment. Maybe if you answer my question, it will help."

"And a little touchy, I see," the man said, but changed his attitude when Lucas gave him a glaring look.

The man raised his hands up, palm forward, saying, "Whoa! Hold on. I ain't wanting no trouble with you, not after what I saw you do."

Lucas lowered his hands and looked directly at the man. "And just what did I do, and why did I do it?"

The man looked down at the floor and said, trying to change the subject, "Are you hungry? I'm starved and I sure could use a cup of strong coffee."

Before Lucas could respond, the man stood up and went to the cell door and called out, "Hey, out there! Can a man get some coffee and a bite to eat, or are we just supposed to starve to death?"

A metal door at the end of the cells opened with the hinges squealing from a lack of oil, and a tall, heavyset man with a badge pinned to his shirt, walked in and stared at the two men. He looked at Lucas and said, "So, you're awake, are ya? I'm bettin' you've got the headache of all headaches. Never saw a man with a head as hard as your 'n."

The black man stepped over and stopped a couple of feet from the bars and said, "Mister jailer-man, sir. Do you suppose we can get some coffee and some breakfast?"

"Name's Seth. Seth Barnes. I'm the deputy sheriff, so keep your eyes and head down when you speak to me, boy."

Anger immediately filled the eyes of the black man and his jaw clamped shut. "I'm no, boy. I'm a free man. But out of respect for that badge pinned on your shirt, I'm asking, politely, can we have some coffee and something to eat?"

The deputy stared at the black man with contempt in his eyes, but grinned and said, "Shore. I'll get right to it, your highness."

Before he left, the deputy looked at Lucas and said, "You boys will be going to see the judge this afternoon, so I suggest you make yourself presentable."

Lucas looked around the cell and saw no water jug or bowl to wash in. "How am I supposed to clean up when there is no soap or water? And I don't have any clean clothes to change into."

"Not my problem," the deputy said as he left the cell area, slamming the door with a bang.

Lucas had wanted to ask the deputy the same questions he'd asked the black man, but he was gone before any questions could be asked.

The black man went back to his bunk and sat down, then said, "Don't get your hopes up about us getting any coffee or breakfast – or you being able to clean up some. He has a reputation of – how can I put it? They say his compassion for prisoners is less than, none."

Lucas' headache had subsided a little and the fuzziness left his eyes. He chuckled and said, "So… I guess I won't make the best impression on the judge, will I?"

The black man said, "Don't reckon you will, but I doubt it will make much difference how you're dressed. Judge Sizemore, looks at what he considers, criminals, about the same way the deputy does."

Lucas was about to ask his questions, again, when the outer door clanged open and the deputy, followed by a black woman carrying a large bag and a tray, came into the cell area. The deputy had a scowl on his face as he unlocked the cell door. "Seems like you have an angel lookin' after you."

The woman walked in and sat the bag and tray on the black man's cot, then leaned down and asked, "Are you alright?"

"I'm fine, honey," he said with a smile. "Thank you for coming."

"Come on, lady, we ain't got all day…" deputy Barnes snarled.

She turned and looked at Lucas and said, pointing at the black man, "He's here, thanks to you," then hurried out of the cell.

When the door closed, Lucas asked, "What was that all about? Where are we, who are you, and why is she angry with me? Did we tangle or something?"

The tray contained a pot of coffee and thick sandwiches made from ham and fried eggs.

As they ate their sandwiches and drank the coffee, the man said, "My name is Rufus Dogwood and that was my wife, Sara, who brought the food and clean clothes for me. She said what she did because of what happened."

Lucas got a puzzled look on his face and said, "I don't understand."

"We're in St. Louis, Missouri, and I play piano at the Rivers Edge Saloon. I had just taken a break when you came staggering in and walked up to the bar and demanded a bottle of whiskey. The bartender took one look at you and told you to leave, but you said, no, not without a bottle of whiskey. The bartender looked at Ace Bellew and Able Crew, the bouncers, and nodded his head."

Rufus took a sip of coffee, then resumed. "You looked pretty much like you do now, filthy and ragged, like you'd been run over by a herd of wild horses or cattle, and I'm guessing the two bouncers thought you'd be easy pickings. But boy, oh, howdy, did you prove them wrong. Even as drunk as you were, you lit into them like a wild banshee. It was a fight to be seen. And in the excitement of the fight, several men who'd had a little too much to drink, decided to join the fracas."

Rufus stopped long enough to take another bite of his sandwich, then chased it with a sip of coffee. "They were overpowering you by sheer numbers, but still you kept fighting and in the heat of the moment, I was overcome with anger about the odds and jumped in and tried to help you."

Lucas swallowed the mouthful of sandwich, then took a drink of his coffee, feeling the warm liquid travel down his insides. "So, what happened then?"

"One of them pulled a knife and yelled, "Let's hang the drunken bastard and gut the slave!""

Lucas sat his cup down and stared at the man, unable to believe what he was hearing.

"Well-sir, you got a look in your eyes and you pulled your knife and motioned for them to come to you. I broke a bottle and pointed the jagged edge toward them. Being gutted didn't sound appealing to me."

A little of it was beginning to come back to Lucas and he nodded his head.

"By the time the sheriff and Deputy Barnes came running in, three of them were laying on the floor, groaning and bleeding. And when the sheriff tried to overpower you, you cut him, too – and I don't know whether he made it or not because Deputy Barnes began hitting you on the head with a club, which just seemed to make you, madder. You were like some whirling dervish. Someone hit me on the head from behind, and I woke up here in jail, with you."

It all came flooding back to Lucas' brain. He hadn't gone in there to cause a fight. He just wanted another bottle of liquor to help keep the memories of losing Crying Dove from his mind.

Try as hard as he could, he couldn't remember how long it had been – far too many bottles of whiskey had passed his lips.

Instinctively, he reached for the small sack of gold he remembered keeping in the left pocket of his pants, and found the pocket, empty.

So, this is how it ends, Lucas thought to himself as he sat his empty coffee cup on the floor, then lay back down on the cot.

TWO

Washington Sizemore, woke up in a surly mood. His tete-ta-tete with Molly Gordon, the dancehall girl he kept on the side, had not gone well. He'd drank too much and she had turned him out, saying, "Go home and sleep it off."

His wife, Martha had not been affectionate, either, and locked the bedroom door. His back hurt from sleeping on the couch and he had a terrible headache, along with bouts of uncontrollable shaking.

When he entered the courtroom, it was packed solid, with people standing around the back wall. Three men had died and the sheriff, Randal Grimes was in serious condition.

The judge climbed the four steps up to where he dropped down in his chair and looked down at Deputy Barnes, who stood looking up at him. "Are the prisoners here?" he asked, pressing his fingers to his temples.

"Just outside the door, Your Honor," Barnes told him.

"Bring them in," he said, looking at the papers in front of him.

When Deputy Barnes led the two men in and stood them in front of the judge, he was appalled at what he saw. Rufus Dogwood, who he knew to be the piano player at the Rivers Edge Saloon, was dressed much better than the white man standing next to him, which did not set well with him. He thought himself to be a fair and just man and had no animosities against black people as long as they stayed in their place.

The white man was filthy and he could smell him clear up behind the bench. His clothes were nothing more than rags and were as dirty as the man. He looked down at the papers on his desk and searched for the man's name, but found nothing.

"Do you have a name?" he asked, looking directly at Lucas.

Lucas had come to the conclusion that he was going to die for what he'd done and felt no reason to be civil. "I do," he said, without saying more.

Judge Sizemore shook his head. "This was not the day for nonsense, so would you please share it with us?" he asked.

Lucas looked up at the judge and said, "Why do you need my name? So you can know what to put on my headstone?"

The judge rubbed his temples, again, then said, "It is customary for me to know a man's name so I know who I am dealing with. So, once more, please state your name for the court records."

"Lucas Penny," he told him.

"Are either of you represented by council?" the judge asked.

When both of them shook their heads, no, he said, "Very well. I will deal with you one at a time."

Judge Sizemore lifted the paper up, and read the charges. "Mister Penny, you are charged with inciting a riot, destroying property and murdering three men, and possibly four, as the sheriff's condition still remains critical. How do you plead?"

"Not guilty. I was just defending myself." Lucas told him, straightening up a little. He doubted it would do him any good to plead, not guilty, but he'd never been a man to go down without a fight.

The judge folded his fingers together and placed them under his chin for a moment as he considered the man's answer. He then lowered his hands and looked down at Rufus, then picked up another piece of paper and read from it. "Rufus Dogwood, you are charged with destroying property, attacking several white men, causing pain and misery to them, plus, pulling a lethal weapon on them in the form of a broken whiskey bottle, with the intent of doing them bodily harm. How do you, plead?"

Rufus knew how most of the people in St. Louis, felt about black people. They were alright as long as they stayed in their place. He looked up at the judge and said, "Your Honor, I feel I got carried away in the moment, with this man beside me, being out numbered and was fighting a losing battle that he didn't start. I plead insanity for trying to jump in and help him. It wasn't my place to do so, Sir, and I apologize to the court for my behavior. I would like to throw myself onto the mercy of the court, and accept whatever punishment you deem fit, Your Honor."

Even as bad as he was feeling, the judge almost burst out into laughter. Here, a black man, was not only dressed better than the white man, he was also more articulate. But the bottom line was – he was a black man who had struck several white men and raised a broken whiskey bottle against them, which meant, he needed to be punished.

"Step forward, Rufus," the judge said, and when Rufus did as he was told, the judge looked down at him and said, "You've admitted to doing what you knew to be wrong and I have no choice but to see that you are made an example. Rufus Dogwood, for crimes against white men, you are to be remanded to the jail and sentenced to six months of hard labor on the docks."

The judge rapped his gavel on the benchtop, and said to Deputy Barnes. "See that Rufus is returned to the jail. His sentence shall begin tomorrow morning."

The deputy nodded to two men sitting in the front row and they jumped up and took Rufus in hand, shoving him toward the side door.

When he'd been taken away, the judge stared down at the man in front of him and felt a stab of sorrow for him. Whatever brought him to this state must have been devastating, and before pronouncing sentence, he wanted to know what it was. Why he was feeling this way, he wasn't sure. In the past, criminals deserved whatever sentence he decided to give them, but there was something about this man…

"Mister Penny, it is now your turn. You said you were just defending yourself. If you will, please tell us, in your own words, what happened."

Lucas looked around the courtroom and saw all the hostile faces. They wanted to see him dead for what he'd done, and at this moment in time, Lucas couldn't give a damn, one way or another.

"Why should I?" Lucas said, shrugging his shoulders. "It won't make a hill of beans what I say, the verdict will be the same. Look around you, judge. Every man and woman in here wants to see me dead for what I did. I already told you, what I did was in self-defense and as far as I'm concerned, nothing more needs to be said."

Washington Sizemore had been a lawyer before becoming a judge, some six and a half years ago, and in all his years, he'd never come across a man more eager to die than this man. Again, he wondered what brought him to this state?

The judge looked out at the crowded room and saw the looks on their faces and knew the man was right. They wanted justice, as they saw it, which meant, they wanted to see this man strung up by the neck until he was dead.

Just then, a man came into the courtroom and walked directly up to the judge's bench and the judge leaned forward to hear what he had to say. "I was sent to tell you that the sheriff died from the stab wound about twenty minutes, ago."

Judge Sizemore leaned back and watched as the man turned and left the courtroom. As far as he was concerned, this last piece of information sealed Lucas Penny's fate.

He cleared his throat and said, "Mister Penny, I have just been informed that the sheriff has died from your stab wound."

There was an audible gasp and a lot of whispering.

"I'm going to disregard the fighting and destruction of property and get right down to the four counts of murder."

He looked down at the calendar on his benchtop and said, "I sentence you to be hanged by the neck until you are dead. Sentence will be carried out six months from today. In the meantime, you will serve at hard labor on the docks, alongside Rufus Dogwood, until the day of the hanging."

With that, he banged his gavel on the benchtop and said, "Court is adjourned."

Deputy Barnes grinned as he led Lucas away. This man had done him a favor and was going to be hung for it. For over a year now, he had been trying to come up with some way of getting rid of the sheriff so he could step up and take his place. The man was a sniveling piece of trash. He was an order taker, plain and simple and didn't deserve the title of sheriff. And now that he was dead, the title would become his – and once he was officially the sheriff, he would show them what being the sheriff of St. Louis was all about.

THREE

Lucas had been allowed to take a bath, and had been given someone's hand-me-down clothes, which fit his skeletal frame like a gunnysack. Rufus' wife, Sara had been ordered to cut Lucas' hair, right down to the skull, and shave off his beard.

"I want him to look like the criminal he is," Seth Barnes told her.

Each morning, around five, Rufus and Lucas were rousted out of bed and shackled, then taken by wagon to the docks, where they spent the next fourteen hours, doing whatever manual labor anyone needed done.

At the end of the day, they were marched to the river, with ropes tied around their necks. They were told to wade into the river, fully dressed and wash as best as they could. They were then, taken to the back of a restaurant and sat in the alley as they ate their one meal of the day.

By the time they were allowed to fall onto their bunks, it was nearly ten o'clock at night. At five o'clock the next morning, it would start all over again.

They were five weeks into their sentence and were walking down the dock, headed for their next job of unloading a ship that had just came in. It was the first time they'd been able to talk during the day. And normally, by the time they were back to their cell, they were too tired to talk.

Lucas told Rufus how sorry he was that things had turned out the way they had for him.

Rufus just nodded his head and was ready to let it go at that, but instead, he said, "Lucas, you are the only white man I've ever had any respect for and the first one I am proud to call, my friend. I believe those rednecks got what they deserved, and I've been thinking on how to keep your neck from stretching a rope."

"Come up with anything?" Lucas asked with a grin.

"Well-sir, I've thought of several things, but each one of them seemed to be filled with holes, if you know what I mean."

Lucas knew exactly what Rufus was talking about. He too had been trying to come up with a plan to escape. He had no desire to be hung. Yes, he had been wrong for going in the place, especially as drunk as he was, having been thrown out of a saloon just down the street. But soaking his brain with alcohol was the only way to keep from thinking about Crying Dove. As far as he was concerned, it was his fault she had died such a humiliating death. He should have gone out in the forest with her that day – guarded her - protected her.

Since the trial and no alcohol to fog his thinking, he'd come to realize that it hadn't been his fault, or hers. Things had been going smoothly for some time and they had no reason to think there would be any trouble.

He also knew that living in the high country, trouble could come from any direction, on any given day. Indians weren't the only things they needed to keep an eye out, for. There were, bears, wolves, mountain lions, and a host of other critters that could attack a person at any given moment.

He still missed and thought about Crying Dove almost every day, but moping around feeling angry or sorry for himself, wasn't the answer. Proof of that was right here in front of him. Crawling into a bottle of whiskey and staying there for God only knew how long, was definitely not the answer. And coming to St. Louis, or any other big city, wasn't the answer, either.

"Yeah, me too," Lucas said.

Rufus looked at his friend and said, "Don't you worry none. I'll think of something,"

"Knock off the talkin'!" the burly guard said, poking Rufus in the back with the butt of his rifle.

Two months later, on a Sunday, when Sara came to visit Rufus, they spent some time, huddled together, talking quietly, and when she left, Rufus waited until they were alone in the cell before he approached Lucas with a smile on his face. "Sara has a plan," he said. "And I'm thinking it's a good one."

They talked, long into the night, trying to nail down the small details.

FOUR

It was five days later before they had a chance to implement their plan. Sara was already on the far side of the Mississippi River and had been there for the past three days – waiting with horses and supplies for their journey.

The ship they were helping to unload, had three lifeboats but each one was too large to be helpful. Getting them into the water would be a long process, so they had been dismissed. They were also discouraged by the fact that they could find nothing aboard that would float – at least, nothing small enough for their needs.

"You'll be stayin' on ta help load the ship as the captain wants ta leave at first light," the guard told them when the ship had been unloaded.

Both Rufus and Lucas gave a sigh. That would take them well past midnight to get the ship loaded – another day passing them by.

It was just after one in the morning when Rufus came up alongside Lucas and whispered, "I think I've found a way."

"I'm all ears," Lucas responded.

"We'll be loading a big stack of hard maple within the hour," Rufus said with a grin.

"So?" Lucas whispered.

"Doncha know, hard maple floats like a duck on the water. We can use it like a float to help us cross the river," Rufus told him.

For some time, now, the two guards had been passing a bottle back and forth and were not doing a good job of watching them.

On one of their trips down to load the cargo net with the lumber, Lucas and Rufus set four pieces of hard maple to the side, hoping that, very soon, they would find a chance to make their escape.

By close to three o'clock, the guards were nodding off and Lucas said, "It's time."

With the pieces of wood, they found near the stacks of lumber, they walked up and clubbed the guards on the head, as the other men who worked the docks, stood by. They'd come to like Lucas and Rufus and watched as the two men tossed the maple boards into the river, then jumped in and began swimming across the now darkened Mississippi River.

As soon as they were out of sight, the men went back to loading the ship as though nothing had happened.

It was very dark out and even if someone had been looking for men swimming in the river, they would more than likely not been able to see them. The Mississippi River was murky at best and loaded with things floating downstream – things like, logs and such.

The current of the Mississippi River was strong and drove Lucas and Rufus a good way downstream. Normally a good swimmer could make the swim in, between thirty and forty-five minutes, but with the existing current, they made the western shore almost an hour later and three-quarters of a mile, downstream from where Sara was supposed to be waiting.

It was still dark when they climbed up on the grassy bank and lay, panting. Rufus looked over at Lucas and began laughing.

"What's so funny?" Lucas asked.

"It worked! We made it!" Rufus cried out.

Lucas climbed to his feet and said, "We're not out of the woods, yet. C'mon, we have some hiking to do. I'll bet Sara is beginning to think we're never coming."

Indeed, Sara paced the riverbank, day and night, watching for them to emerge from the river, only to be disappointed each day.

When they finally did get to the meeting spot, they came from the wrong direction and she was both happy and confused.

"It was the current," Rufus told her. "It took us close to a mile downstream."

Sara smiled and said, "No matter. You have finally come, and that is all that matters."

She pulled some clothes out of a sack and said, "Here, I brought you some clothes. You can't go around looking like escaped criminals."

After getting into the dry clothes, Lucas put his foot in the stirrup and swung his leg over his horse, saying, "We need to put some distance between us and St. Louis. I doubt if those people back across the river are too happy about now."

"I have sandwiches we can eat while we ride. I'm guessing you two are hungry after what you've been through - which will be a story our children and grandchildren will want to hear," Sara said, climbing onto her horse.

Rufus jerked his head around and asked, "Are you trying to tell me something?"

Sara chuckled and said, "No, silly. I'm just saying, someday."

The sun was coming over the horizon when they reached the far side of West St. Louis and Lucas suggested they keep on riding.

"My horse is getting tired," Rufus said, shrugging his shoulders.

"So is mine," Lucas said. "But this is no place to stop. I have no doubt, people will be looking for us, right soon, like."

After swallowing the last bite of his sandwich, Lucas said, "Maybe we can find someone to trade with us?"

They were several miles west of St. Louis, and the horses had slowed down to a walk and were beginning to lather up.

Off to the right, Lucas saw what appeared to be a large farm. "Let's try this farm. Maybe he has some horses he'll trade to us."

Rufus hauled up his horse, causing Lucas and Sara to also stop their horses. "What's wrong?" Lucas asked.

Rufus rubbed the back of his neck and said, "I don't think we should go with you."

"It's because you're black, isn't it?" Lucas said.

"Yes-sir, it is," Rufus said. "If a black man and a black woman goes riding in there with lathered up horses, what do you suppose he will think?"

"That you're run-a-ways. And if I'm with you, he'll think I'm some kind of slave dealer, or I'm helping you escape," Lucas conceded.

"And we don't know which way that man over there, believes. He could be on our side, or he could be a member of the Klan, which would set another bunch on our trail besides the law."

Lucas got a frown on his face and asked, "The Klan? Are you talking about the Klu-Klux-Klan?"

"I am," Rufus said. "They're real active in this part of the country. And I'd just as soon not have a run-in with them, if you get my drift?"

In the end, they unsaddled all three horses. Rufus and Sara stayed behind, hidden in a small group of elm trees while Lucas rode up to the farm, leading the two unsaddled horses.

The house was a large, two-story affair, and the barn was painted bright red. The area was clean and neat looking. There were close to a dozen horses in the corral and Lucas rode over to the fence and stepped down, tying the horses to the fence.

Lucas had just finished when a large man in Levi pants and a work shirt walked out of the barn and headed toward him. "Mornin'. Looks like you've been doing some hard riding."

Lucas turned and walked over to the man with his hand stretched out. "Good morning. Name's Patrick Boone, from over south of Pekin, Illinois, and you're right, I have been riding hard and I'm in need of your help if you're so obliged to."

The man shook Lucas' hand and said, "Could be, but first, a man would need to know the particulars."

Lucas hung his head for a moment for effect, then looked up and stared the man in the eyes and said, "Some might say I'm a criminal, while others would think otherwise. You see, my younger brother, Matthew, was sweet on Caroline Waters but with the Waters thinking they're better than most folks around Pekin, they look down on us Boones and told him to stay away from her. Course, I'm sure you know how young people in love are. They don't give a hoot what other folks say – not even kinfolk."

Lucas gave a sigh, then continued. "Well, the long and the short of it is, Mathew and Caroline sneaked out and met down at Miller's Pond.

"And Caroline told me later, they were sparking, some, when Clevis, Caroline's brother rode up and saw 'em. Well-sir, according to what Caroline told me, he pulled out his pistol and shot my brother, Matthew, then hauled Caroline home. And when their father found out, Caroline said he gave her a beating."

Lucas shook his head. "Never much believed in hitting women, and I was awful mad about Clevis shooting my brother. And after Caroline ran away and come to our place and told us what happened, I was fit to be tied, and rode over to the Waters place and called Clevis out, telling him to be wearing a gun."

"And did he come out - wearing a gun?" the farmer asked.

"He did, and his pa and two brothers came with him – all of them, armed."

"What happened, then?" the farmer asked.

"Well-sir, I looked at them and said, I ain't got no truck with any of you except the one who killed my brother – so step aside and let me get on with the business I come here to do, which didn't mean a hill of beans to them cause ole man Waters said, "You have a beef with one of us, you have all of us to deal with. And with that, he pulled his pistol and commenced shooting."

Lucas could see he had the farmer hooked and he continued. "I yanked my pistol from my holster and shot back. I shot ole man Waters, first, then turned my gun and shot Clevis. And while the other two were fumbling around, trying to get their guns out of their holsters, I jumped on my horse and lit a shuck – and I've been riding hard ever since. I've got a bit of a lead on them, but I know they're still on my trail. I don't have much money and I know my horses are plumb tuckered out, but I'd be much obliged if we could do some trading."

"Name's Howard Levine, and that's some story. Can't say I've ever heard better. Don't know if it's the truth or some made-up lie – but it is some story, and I'm inclined to believe you."

Howard looked over the three horses Lucas had to offer and said, "They look tired from being ridden hard, but otherwise, they look sound."

Howard walked over to where Lucas stood, holding his breath, and said, "Pick out any three of the ones in the corral, and the best of luck to you. If what you told me is true, I know I would have done the same thing, in your place."

Lucas rode into the stand of trees, riding an Appaloosa mare, leading a paint and a black, and when he slid down, Rufus looked at him and said, "Don't know what you did or what you said, but it must have been powerful convincing."

"You wouldn't believe me if I told you," Lucas said with a wide grin.

Just prior to the sun disappearing beyond the horizon, Lucas led them into a stand of trees that had a small stream of clear water running through it. "I think it will be safe to spend the night here."

Lucas was surprised when Rufus put together a fire that had precious little smoke and Sara found a branch and swept the area clean, then commenced to fix a meal from the things she had in a bag hanging from the pommel of her saddle.

When Rufus saw the surprised look on Lucas' face, he said, "Didn't always play the piano in saloons."

Lucas looked at his new friend and said, "I'd be most interested to hear the whole story."

The next several weeks was spent putting miles and miles between themselves and St. Louis, along with anyone who might still be chasing them.

They stayed clear of towns since they had no money to spend, anyway. They did, however, steal a chicken or two, here and there, along with raiding a few gardens for vegetables from farmers who seemed to have plenty.

Lucas watched their back trail, and after a while, he figured they had given up and turned back. At least he hoped that was the case.

FIVE

Seth Barnes was livid with anger when he found out his two prisoners had escaped. He paced the floor of the sheriff's office, grinding his teeth and clenching and unclenching his fists.

The following morning, he went to the mayor's office and was sworn in as the new sheriff – then immediately, hired a deputy and took a leave of absence.

"I won't have it on my conscience or my record that I allowed two prisoners, to escape. I'll be leaving my deputy in charge while I go find them and bring them back, Mayor," Seth said, shaking his head.

"How long do you think it will take?" the mayor asked.

"Not sure, but I'm hoping it won't take long. Those two have put a dirty mark on my record and I won't have it, even if I have to chase 'em clear to the end of the earth!" Seth yelled, causing the mayor to sit back in his chair.

"When will you be leaving?" the mayor asked, obviously afraid of the new sheriff.

"First thing in the morning," Seth said, picking up his hat and setting it on his head.

When the new sheriff was gone, the mayor gave a sigh and took a handkerchief from his back pocket and mopped the sweat on his forehead. He was glad Seth was leaving town, in pursuit of the two escaped prisoners - and hoped it would take him, months – maybe years to catch them. The man was not, in his opinion, the kind of man the people of St. Louis wanted as sheriff. He was arrogant, cruel, and had a bad temper. During Seth's time as the deputy, he'd had far too many prisoners die when he was on duty, because of accidents, as he called them – or attempts to escape.

The mayor leaned back in his chair and nodded his head. The new deputy, Kyle Holcombe, was a good man – a deacon in his church. He wasn't married, which in the mayor's mind, was a good thing. When dealing with criminals, he wouldn't have the need to worry about a wife or children. He was a big man – six foot five, and he could handle himself when the need arose. He would make a good, acting sheriff, and who knew, maybe...

The following morning, Seth rode his horse onto the ferry, leading a mule loaded down with camping supplies and food enough to last a month, or more, if he was careful. He stood on the bow of the ferry, watching as they crossed the river. On this narrow part of the Mississippi, it would take only twenty minutes or so to make the crossing, then he would begin his pursuit.

SIX

After leaving St. Louis they made their way, west, stopping here and there, along the way, hoping to pick up a little work, to put some money in their pockets. Rufus and Lucas did manual labor and from time-to-time Sara got some housecleaning jobs.

They had been on the road close to two weeks when they rode into Kansas City, Missouri. Kansas City is split into two towns, the east side in Missouri and the west side in Kansas.

"I think we should stop here long enough to build up some money. We're going to need a good-size poke to buy what we need, once we reach, Denver, which will be our jumping off point," Lucas told them.

"We have some put away, now," Sara said. "Why can't we go on to Denver and see about some work, there? Wouldn't that make more sense?"

"That sounds like the reasonable thing to do, but there is little or no work available, there," Lucas told her. "Denver is a bustling city, but every man-jack going west through Denver is looking for work – which means, with so many men looking for work, if you happen to get hired by someone, they are going to pay you half, or less, than the job is worth. Denver is a dog-eat-dog, city, right now. I think it's better if we stop here and see if we can find some work."

Rufus suggested if they were going to hang around Kansas City for a while, then maybe it should be in the Kansas side, which made sense, if anyone was still following them.

"I doubt anyone would follow us this far, but I think you're right – the other side of the border might be the best thing to do," Lucas agreed.

Kansas City, Kansas proved to be a little smaller that her other half in Missouri, but they weren't discouraged. Sara was getting tired of sleeping on the ground and not being able to take a bath on a regular basis, so they decided to look for a rooming house they could afford.

They found one on the far western part of town, called, Ma Perkins – Clean rooms and three squares a day – seventy-five cents a day.

As it turned out, Ma Perkins was a widow woman who had a big house and she had several vacant rooms.

She was in her fifties, and still full of life. Three widowed men lived there on mostly, a permanent basis – which Ma Perkins encouraged.

Trading labor for free room and board for her and Rufus, Sara hired on to help Ma Perkins with the cleaning and laundry, leaving only the cooking for Ma Perkins to do.

Less than half a mile back toward the city, Rufus found work as a piano player in a saloon called, Big Mike's – Whiskey, beer, girls, and poker.

The place did a lively business and Big Mike thought music might liven things up, even more than it already was.

Lucas also found work at Big Mike's, but not as an employee of Big Mike. Lucas made him a proposition he couldn't refuse. Lucas told him, "Poker games are okay, but the house only makes a small cut – and from what I've observed, the poker games don't amount to much,"

Big Mike was just like his name inferred. He stood six feet four inches in his stocking feet, and pushed the scales close to the three-hundred-pound mark.

"So, what's your point?" he asked.

"Faro," Lucas said, nodding his head up and down. Faro brings in more money and the house gets a bigger split.

"You a Faro dealer, are you? Cause you don't look much like a card player," Big Mike said, eyeing Lucas, who was dressed in denim pants and a wool shirt.

Lucas laughed and said, "These are my riding clothes. Gets mighty dusty out there. If we can make a deal, I'll show up, dressed appropriately."

Even though Lucas hadn't answered Big Mike's question about his ability to deal Faro, they came to an agreement. Lucas would furnish the cards and run the game, giving Big Mike, forty percent of the take.

Lucas rode into town and found a church that sold used clothes and found a suit that almost fit him. The coat was fine, but the legs were too long. For an extra quarter, the minister's wife offered to hem them.

She was close to sixty and a bit on the homely side, but Lucas could care less about her looks. He just wanted his pants to fit.

She stood him on a chair to measure the pant legs and when she did, she wasn't very ladylike about it, causing Lucas to look around to see if her husband was watching.

Luckily, he wasn't.

"You come back anytime you need your pants, hemmed," she said with a giggle.

Lucas rode back toward the boarding house, promising himself never to go there again.

Ma Perkins put on a good spread and Lucas ate his fill for the first time in a long while.

The next several weeks went by quickly and Lucas was building up a reputation of running a fair game and his table was filled, every night. Between the piano playing and the men dancing with the girls, which led to drinking and whatever else the girls could dream up, and the Faro games, Big Mike was making more money than he ever had.

"It was my lucky day, when you two showed up," he told them.

Between his salary and the tips, the drunks would give him to play their favorite songs, Rufus was also building up a tidy sum.

The money had been so good, Lucas had even given thought to staying here, but in the end, knew he wouldn't be happy until he got back up into high country. He was a mountain man and that's where he belonged.

He'd gone so far as to checking with Sara and Rufus to see if they thought they had enough money to head for Denver?

"Gettin' anxious to see them mountains, are you?" Rufus asked with a grin.

"Something like that," Lucas admitted.

"How much you think we need?" Rufus asked.

Lucas thought for a moment, then said, "A hundred or more, I would guess."

Sara, who was the keeper of her and Rufus' money, said, "We got close to a hundred and fifty."

Lucas nodded his head and said, "We still have the weekend, which is when Rufus and I make most of our money. So, how about we leave first thing, Monday morning?"

Sara agreed to have their things packed and ready to go. Now, all she had to do was tell Ma Perkins she would be leaving.

"And we'll need to inform Big Mike," Lucas said.

Rufus shook his head and chuckled. "Don't think he's going to like us leaving, much. He's gotten used to the money we've been bringing in."

"He'll find someone else," Lucas said with a grin.

Indeed, Big Mike was upset when Lucas told him they were leaving and he protested quite loudly. "You can't leave, now! Do you realize how much money we'll all be losing? I won't let you go! No! I forbid it!"

Lucas grinned and said, "You'll find another piano player and a new Faro dealer. You may be down for a couple of days, but I doubt it will be longer than that."

Big Mike nodded his head and sighed. "Gonna miss you boys. If you're ever back this way and want to pick up some money, you just come see me."

It was late, Saturday night, an hour or so before closing time. There were still three hangers-on at the Faro table and Lucas had just told them he would be closing the game, soon, which amounted to some friendly grumbling. "I'll be here tomorrow to get my money back," one of them said.

But before Lucas could respond, a man stepped up and said, "Don't worry yourselves about coming back, tomorrow, because he won't be here."

Lucas looked over and saw Seth Barnes pointing a pistol at him. "Took me a while to track you down, but I've finally caught up to you, and now, you and your friend are comin' with me, back to St. Louis."

Lucas looked toward the piano and saw Rufus sitting, tied and gagged. He looked around for Big Mike, but he was nowhere to be seen.

The men at the Faro table, quickly disappeared, leaving just Lucas and Seth Barnes.

Lucas saw the sheriff's badge on Seth's shirt and said, "I see you finally got the sheriff's job."

"I did. Thanks to you," Seth said with a snarl on his lips and an evil look in his eyes.

The memory of that night was clear in his brain, and he remembered men attacking him with knives and he'd fought back. Sadly, one of the men he'd killed was the sheriff. But the man was trying to overpower him, and in his drunken stupor...

Lucas wasn't carrying a gun and he wasn't about to make trouble for Seth. The man would just as well shoot him so he wouldn't have to hire someone to help him take him and Rufus back to St. Louis.

"Put your hands behind your back, Penny," Seth said, pointing the pistol in Lucas' direction.

Lucas did as he was told and felt the cold steel clamp down against his wrists.

He was then marched over to where Rufus was sitting, tied to a chair. Lucas looked around and saw that, except for the two bartenders and the girls who worked the bar, the place was empty – including the owner, Big Mike.

"I guess the bartenders or the girls will tell Big Mike what happened," Rufus said to Lucas when they were standing next to each other.

Lucas was about to respond when they heard, "Tell me what?" Big Mike asked as he came from the back of the saloon.

When he saw the place was empty and Lucas and Rufus were standing off to the side, with handcuffs on them, he asked, "What's going on, here?"

"Who are you to be askin'?" Seth said, stepping in Big Mike's direction – his hand close to the pistol on his hip.

"Name's Big Mike, and I own this place and these two men work for me. Now, like I asked, what's going on, here?"

Seth grinned and said, "For your information, you hired yourself a couple of escaped prisoners – criminals, who were bein' held on murder charges. Four murders, as a matter of fact. They escaped several months back and I been trackin' them all the way from St. Louis, Missouri. I'll be takin' 'em back to finish out their sentences. You got any objections to that?"

Big Mike looked at Rufus, then over to Lucas, then back to Seth, then said, "Not if the charges are true, but my gut tells me there's more to this story than you're telling me.

Big Mike looked back at Lucas and asked, "Is what this man says, true?"

Lucas shook his head from side to side and said, "Yes, and no."

Seth, suddenly didn't like the way things were going and he stepped between Big Mike and his prisoners. "If you ain't their mouthpiece, then you got no authority to be askin' any questions. So, back off!"

Seth was bristled up like a bull gorilla ready to fight, which had always buffaloed people in the past, but to his surprise, not this time.

Big Mike reached out and grabbed Seth by the front of his shirt and lifted him off the floor with one hand, and shoved the end of his pistol in Seth's face with the other hand.

"Now, you hear me, and hear me good, sheriff, or whoever you are. You're no longer in Missouri. You're in Kansas and you have no jurisdiction here. And it just so happens, I do represent these men, and I want to hear their side of it."

Still holding Seth six inches off the floor, with the barrel of a pistol pressed against his cheek, Big Mike yelled, "Harlan! Dan!"

And like magic, two burly men showed up.

Big Mike grinned at Seth and said, "These two young men work for me as my personal bodyguards and should

I give them a nod… well, all I can say is, they've been known to make men disappear. You get my meaning?"

Seth looked at the two men who looked like either of them could down a bull elephant with just one blow, and nodded his head, yes.

"Now," Big Mike told him. "I'm going to put you back down on the floor and when I do, I want you to walk over to one of those tables nearby, and sit down and be very quiet while I talk to Lucas and Rufus. Shake your head, yes, if you're going to do as I ask? Otherwise, I'll turn you over to Harlan and Dan. So, what's it going to be?"

Seth nodded his head, yes, and was stood back on his feet and the pistol was pulled away from his face.

Without a word, Seth walked over and sat down at one of the nearby tables and placed his hands on top of it.

Big Mike looked at Dan and asked, "Dan, would you please get this gentleman a cup of coffee? He seems to need it."

"Yes-sir," Dan said, then headed for the bar area.

Big Mike walked over to Seth and rummaged through his vest pockets and removed a key, then went back to Lucas and Rufus. He removed the handcuffs and threw them on a nearby table.

"Now, why don't the three of us go to the kitchen where we can get a bite to eat and you can tell me your side of the story.

When Lucas finished telling his side of the story, with Rufus filling in the parts Lucas wasn't all that clear on, Big Mike finished off what was left in his coffee, then said, "As far as I see it, you boys were a victim of circumstances. Maybe, Lucas here wasn't as polite as he should have been when he ordered the bottle of whiskey, but then, the men in the bar had no business interfering, either. And as far as the killings are concerned, that was purely self-defense. Clear as clear can be."

He refilled his coffee cup, took a sip, then said, "Now, about the two of you jumping ship, so to speak, well, I think I would have done the same thing had I been in your shoes. You were up against a stacked deck."

Big Mike reached in his pocket and withdrew a large wad of money. He counted out five hundred dollars and gave Rufus and Lucas, each, two hundred and fifty dollars.

"What's this for?" Lucas asked. "You don't owe us any money."

"Traveling money," he said. "You're going to need to put some distance between here and wherever you're headed, and you're going to need to do it as quickly as you can. I suggest, the stagecoach."

"But…" Lucas protested to a raised hand.

"Consider it my contribution to the fairness of law and order," Big Mike said with a grin. "Now get out of here. And go out the back door. There's more than likely a stagecoach headed west sometime after daylight, so you don't have any time to waste."

"What about?" Rufus tried to ask, but Big Mike raised his hand and said, "Don't fret none about him. I won't kill him, but I'll let the boys play with him for a week or so and put the fear in him, of what will happen to him if he continues to chase after you"

SEVEN

While it wasn't the most pleasant way to travel, the stagecoach was the fastest. Traveling across Kansas on the way to Denver may have been as flat as the bottom of a frying pan, it was also very dusty and they had to keep the window covers pulled down most of the time. It did rain, twice during their ten-day trip that cost them, sixty dollars and thirty cents, each. Meals at the stations where the horses were changed, came at the high price of one dollar per meal, each.

The man who sold them their tickets told them the trip usually took ten to eleven days, and warned them, "The stagecoach has been robbed six times this month, already, so, hide your money if you have any.

Lucas hid his money inside the top part of his boots, while Rufus did the same, which included Sara's money, too.

"Outrageous!" Sara complained to the woman who served them beef stew, at the first stagecoach station they came to, some six hours after leaving Kansas City. "It doesn't cost more than fifteen cents to make this meal, and you charged us a whole dollar. That's the same as robbing folks of what little money they have!"

The woman nodded her gray-haired head and said, "I couldn't agree with you more, but that's the fee the stage line set and that's the price we have to charge. My husband gets thirty a month to run this station, along with a place for us to live, and my salary comes from a portion of the sale of meals. I'm sorry for your displeasure. I hope you at least, enjoy the stew."

When the woman had gone, Sara relinquished her attitude, a little and said, "The stew isn't as good as I make, but it's tolerable."

Lucas and Rufus, both laughed, inside, but outside, they just nodded their heads.

Just a few miles from the Colorado border, and just outside the town that sat on both sides of the border, the coach began to slow down.

It was late afternoon, and they were tired. They were looking forward to a hot bath, a good meal, a drink or two, and a good night's sleep.

Rufus stuck his head out of the window and looked ahead, then pulled it back in, saying, "Two men with masks over their faces and pistols in their hands are sitting on their horses just up ahead, blocking the road."

Lucas was not about to allow a bunch of road robbers to take what didn't belong to them and he drew his pistol and said, "I'm not giving up my money, how about you, Rufus?"

Rufus pulled his pistol and looked at Sara. "Lay down on the floor of the coach and don't move til I tell you it's safe."

Without an argument, Sara did as Rufus told her to do.

The drivers of the stages were told by their bosses, to not try and play hero if they were threatened. "Give them the money, then report it to the first sheriff you can find, and send us a wire, telling us what happened."

These orders came directly from the head office. They would turn the information over to the Pinkerton Agency, who handled these kinds of things.

The man riding shotgun, leaned down and yelled for the passengers to hear. "Robbers up ahead. Don't do anything foolish and you'll be all right. Give them whatever they ask for, then turn in a claim to the head office. Remember, don't do anything foolish and no one will get hurt."

Lucas looked at Rufus and said, "Sounds to me like someone might be in cahoots with the holdup men."

"Best we keep an eye on him too," Rufus replied.

The stage came to a halt and they heard one of the robbers call out, "Everybody out of the coach with your hands in the air, and don't try anything foolish, unless you think this is a good day to die."

Lucas looked down at Sara and said, "Stay where you are." He then looked at Rufus and said, "You cover the driver and the man riding shotgun, and I'll handle the two men trying to rob us."

Rufus nodded his head and said, "You say when."

The robber's voice came at them, again. "I'm not gonna tell you again to get out of the coach. I'm gonna count to three, then start putting bullet holes in the sides."

"When," Lucas said, as he shoved the door open and jumped out with his pistol blazing.

As Rufus came out of the coach, he looked up and saw the man riding shotgun, raise his rifle and was about to shoot Lucas. Rufus raised his pistol and shot the man, dead center in his chest, knocking him off his seat.

The driver was in the midst of drawing his pistol when Rufus' second bullet drove its way into his forehead, knocking him backward onto the ground, while Lucas disposed of the two robbers, shooting each one before they could get their pistols clear of leather.

Without discussing what needed to be done, they loaded the bodies into the coach and tied one of the horses to the back of the coach. Sara sat next to Rufus, who drove the stagecoach, while Lucas rode the extra horse that had been owned by one of the dead robbers.

The sun was disappearing over the far western mountains when Rufus pulled the stagecoach up and stopped in front of the sheriff's office.

A man of about fifty came out and looked up at Rufus and Sara. Lucas stepped down from his horse and walked up to the sheriff and introduced himself, Rufus and Sara, then told him what happened, paying close attention to the man's reactions.

The sheriff looked at the dead bodies and Lucas gave a sigh of relief when the sheriff said, "I've been suspecting something wasn't right about those robberies. Too many coincidents about robberies happening when the coach was carrying big sums of money."

"You think the coach is carrying a big sum of moncy?" Rufus asked.

"A little over thirty thousand dollars. Payment to the cattle ranchers around here for the beef they sold a few wecks back," he told them.

"Should be in a locked strongbox just under where you've been sitting. It's my guess, ole man Larson, the one who drove the coach, informed his friends when large sums of money was coming in. And I'm betting that if we search his place, and Charlie Mason's place, the man who rode shotgun, we'll find what's left from a bunch of robberies."

Lucas, Rufus and Sara stood by while the sheriff climbed up and retrieved the strongbox from the stagecoach, then followed him to the bank, where the president, himself, opened the box and sure enough, it was filled with money.

"I'm thinking you folks messed up their final haul. There's enough there, along with the other robberies for them to take off for places unknown and live real comfortable like for a good while."

The president of the bank looked at them and asked, "Which one of you gets the reward?"

"Reward? What reward?" Lucas asked.

The bank president chuckled and asked, "Didn't the sheriff tell you? We suspected there were more than one outlaw involved with the robberies, so we placed a five-hundred-dollar reward on each member of the gang that was brought to justice, and I guess what you did amounts to bringing the entire gang to justice. Now, which one of you do I give the money to?"

Lucas did some quick calculating in his head and came up with six hundred and sixty-six dollars and some change for each of them. He looked at the bank president and said, "Give us a second or two to discuss this."

Lucas, Rufus and Sara spent less than five minutes huddled a short distance away from the sheriff and the bank president, before Lucas came back and asked, "That sign in your window for real?"

"If you're talking about the one asking for donations to help build a hospital, then, yes. Why do you ask?"

Lucas grinned and said, "The reward money comes to two thousand dollars and split three ways, well, it's a mite confusing. But if we each take five hundred, that leaves five hundred we can use to donate to the new hospital fund. Can we do that?"

The bank president reached out and shook each of their hands, thanking them for the donation.

While they were having supper with the sheriff, he asked, "How long are you folks going to be in town?"

Rufus laid his knife and fork on the table and said, "We'll be leaving on the next stagecoach headed for Denver."

The sheriff shook his head and said, "That might take a while. You shot and killed the driver and the man riding shotgun, which I know, was in self-defense, but as far as I know, they haven't gotten any replacements, yet."

"How long might that take?" Sara asked.

"Can't rightly say," the sheriff told her. "Drivers and shotgun riders aren't easy to come by. Could be days – could be weeks, even months."

The next morning, as soon as the stagecoach company opened its door, Lucas and Rufus walked in and signed on as driver and shotgun rider – as far as Denver – offering to do it for no pay.

"Once we get to Denver, we'll be moving on. You should have an easier time of finding a new driver, there, rather than here," Lucas told the man who ran the stagecoach office.

An hour later, after a brief instruction on where the way-stations were, Lucas snapped the reins on the six horse's rumps and yelled, "Yee-haw!" Rufus sat next to him with a repeating rifle laying across his legs, while Sara tried to make herself comfortable inside the coach.

"That was nice of him to give our money back we paid for the trip, doncha think?" Rufus asked.

"I guess he figured since we didn't want no salary, he figured it was the least he could do," Lucas said, nodding his head.

Between this free ride to Denver and that money we got for bringing in those outlaws, it's turning out to be a right nice trip," Rufus said, lighting up a cheroot.

It was still a long way to Denver, just under five hundred miles, which they guessed would take them a full eight days.

At the end of the first day, Lucas was tired. He hadn't figured driving six-up for twelve hours would be as hard as it turned out. His hands and arms ached and were having spasms.

"I'll drive tomorrow and you ride shotgun," Rufus told Lucas at the supper table.

Lucas just nodded his head. He was too tired to argue and as soon as he finished eating, he went to the room provided and fell onto the cot, almost asleep before he landed.

The room was meant for two men, and Sara complicated things.

"I'll make you a pallet in the storeroom," the stationmaster's wife said. "I hope that will do," she said.

"Anyplace will be fine," Sara told her. She too, was tired from being shaken up and down and sideways for twelve hours. Riding a stagecoach wasn't as pleasant a way to travel as the ticket tellers made it sound like.

"It's a grand way to travel and see the countryside. It's a pastoral view from sunup to sundown."

"Yeah, right, if you can keep your eyeballs from rolling around in the sockets," Sara said as she looked at the pallet on top of some packing crates.

Lucas and Rufus were awakened by hearing Sara's voice shouting at them, "Rufus! Lucas! Come quick! We're being attacked by Indians!"

The two men slid into their pants and boots, and grabbed their guns as they ran for the front room of the way station.

"I thought Indians didn't like to fight at night. Some kind of belief that if they get killed their souls won't be able to find the happy hunting grounds," Rufus said as they raced into the front room.

"Guess no one told this bunch," Lucas said as he ran to the window and looked out.

Approximately a dozen Indians were riding back and forth in front of the station, firing at them with rifles.

"Where'd they get those rifles?" Rufus asked.

"Why don't you go out there and ask 'em," the stationmaster said.

"Now that's not a bad idea," Rufus said as he opened the door and stepped outside before anyone could stop him.

The stationmaster looked at Lucas and asked, "What's the matter with him? Has he lost his mind? He's a walking dead man."

But to their surprise, when Rufus walked out of the station with his hands out in the open showing no weapon, although he was wearing a pistol, and yelling, "Hey! What in blue blazes are y'all doing here? I was trying to get some sleep and you come in here, yelling and shootin' up the place…"

Confused at seeing a black man, who was yelling at them, the Indians halted their attack and stared at him.

"Who's in charge, here?" Rufus asked, walking up to a brave, whose face, chest and arms were covered with war paint. "You the big chief?"

The Indian looked down at Rufus and studied him. He'd never seen a black man before and he was curious.

"I am called, Strong Buffalo and I am the leader. Who are you and how did you get your skin so, black?"

"Oh, well, about that," Rufus said with a shrug of his shoulders. "You see, there were these Cherokee Indians back in North Carolina who didn't like me much, and tried to kill me by burning me at the stake, but I walked out of that fire and killed them all. But in the end, the fire turned my skin black as coal. I guess you could say I was blessed by the gods."

Strong Buffalo's eyes got wide and he translated what Rufus told him, to his friends, to oohs and aahs.

Strong Buffalo turned back to Rufus and asked, "Do you and your gods protect this place?"

"Even when I am no longer here, the gods that serve me will serve them," Rufus said, crossing his arms across his chest.

From inside, the stationmaster looked at Lucas and asked, "What's he telling them?"

"I don't have the foggiest, but you can bet it's about him being a powerful god or some such, truck," Lucas said, nodding his head. "When it comes to telling tall tales, Rufus Dogwood stands right up there with the likes of Jim Bridger."

The stationmaster didn't know the famous, Jim Bridger, but he'd heard stories. "You don't say?"

"I do. I've heard him tell some whoppers so big that you couldn't dispute them," Lucas said, nodding his head up and down, vigorously.

The stationmaster looked out through the window in time to see the Indians ride away. "Well, I'll be hog-swallowed," he said.

When Rufus came back inside, the stationmaster ran over to him and asked, "What in tarnation did you say to 'em?"

Rufus laid his hand on the man's shoulder and said, "I told him because of the color of my skin, I was blessed by the gods and if he didn't leave and never come back, I would put a curse on him and his people."

"And he believed you?" the stationmaster asked, his eyes wide with disbelief.

"Maybe it was when I turned my finger into fire that convinced him," Rufus said with a wide grin.

"Turned your finger into fire?" The stationmaster was totally confused by now.

Rufus reached into his pocket and pulled out a lucifer and struck it with his thumb and held the flame up just above one of his fingers.

"Told you," Lucas said as he slapped Rufus on the back. "Think it's safe to go back to bed?" he asked.

"They won't ever be coming back here," Rufus said as he headed back toward their sleeping quarters.

The following morning, when Rufus sat down at the breakfast table, the stationmaster's wife sat a large platter in front of Rufus, instead of a plate. It had a large slice of ham, four fried eggs, a good size batch of fried potatoes and a tall stack of hot cakes, smothered with butter and molasses – along with a steaming hot cup of coffee.

"If you want more, you just tell me," she said with a smile.

"Shucks, ma 'am, I'm not even sure I can eat all of this, but I shore do thank you," Rufus said.

In the end, everyone marveled when Rufus finished, and his platter was so clean you almost didn't need to wash it.

EIGHT

Seven days later, Denver loomed up in front of them with the mountains rising into the sky, behind it.

After the four passengers they'd picked up along the way got down and was given their luggage, Lucas turned the stagecoach over to the Denver office.

"Sure you don't want to stay on? I can send you out tomorrow, headed back to where you came from," the man said, tilting his head and smiling.

"Sorry, but I've got other plans," Lucas said, then walked out onto the sidewalk and stopped. Everywhere he looked, people were moving around like a bunch of ants on a mission.

Two blocks down the street, Lucas caught up with Rufus and Sara, who were standing in front of a hotel. Their bags sat at their feet and Rufus had a face full of anger.

"What's wrong?" Lucas asked, knowing the answer, already.

"I think you know the answer," Rufus said with a sigh.

"Sorry," Lucas said, then grinned and said, "It's a lousy hotel, anyway. Follow me, I know of a better place where a person's skin color doesn't matter."

Lucas hailed a man driving a horse drawn cab, and gave him an address, and the fare for taking them, there.

Fifteen minutes later they were standing in front of a huge, two-story house. The sign out next to the front gate, read, ROOM AND BOARD – seven dollars a week.

Lucas led them up to the front door and knocked.

An attractive woman in her early forties opened the door and smiled when she saw Lucas. Both Rufus and Sara looked at the woman and smiled. She was dressed in a white woman's clothes, but she was definitely an Indian.

"Lucas!" the woman said and without any modesty or shame, she threw her arms around his neck and embraced him.

The woman then stepped back and put her hands on his shoulders and asked, "Are you all right? The last time I saw you, you were a mess."

"I was riding the pity train for a while, but I'm fine now," Lucas told her, then continued. "My friends and I need a room for a week. You have anything available?"

The woman smiled and motioned for them to come inside, saying, "If I didn't, for you, I would throw someone out."

Lucas' face looked flushed as they went inside.

The woman turned and looked at Rufus and Sara, and said, "My American name is, Grace Adams. I married a white man ten years ago. He was a miner who did all right for himself, but was killed by a Sioux brave. I came here with the money he left me and bought this house. My Cherokee name is, Awinita, which means, fawn, or, one who is gentle. You may call me by whichever name you choose."

Lucas butted in, saying, "Don't let that gentle part fool you. You cross her and you'll see why she should have been named, madder than a wet hen."

Grace stuck her tongue out at Lucas, then stuck out her hand toward Rufus.

Rufus took her hand and shook it, saying, "My name is Rufus Dogwood and this is my wife, Sara. And as far as what to call you, ma 'am, I think I'll stick to, Grace. Easier to remember and say."

Grace took Sara's hand and said, "I'll bet putting up with these two is a real challenge."

Sara smiled and said, "The stories I could tell."

Both women laughed, then Grace said, "Let me show you to your room – then turned to Lucas and said, "I think you know where your room is."

Lucas blushed and put the tips of his fingers to the brim of his hat, saying, "I think I can remember the way."

Rufus got a puzzled look on his face until it hit his brain. He grinned and winked at Lucas – then picked up the luggage and followed Grace and Sara.

The next several days were filled with buying the things they would need to survive the high country. Lucas was going back to being a mountain man – and although, neither Rufus or Sara had ever seen the Rocky Mountains until now, let alone, trying to live up in the high country, they both agreed this was something they wanted to try.

Lucas had spent several days, describing both the wonders and the hardships, and when he had nothing more to say, they still wanted to give that lifestyle a try.

"Up there, we will truly be, free. Won't be nobody looking down on us or treating us like we're still slaves," Rufus said as his reasoning to become a mountain man.

"And we don't need all the hardships living in the city comes with. We have each other, and that's enough. Of course, you're always a welcome sight, when you happen to be on our part of the mountain," Sara said, resting her hand on Lucas' arm.

Lucas decided against buying a wagon, opting for a horse to ride and a pack mule to carry his necessaries.

On the sixth morning after arriving in Denver, Lucas, Rufus and Sara said their goodbyes to Grace and headed northwest.

"Whenever you get back to Denver, you'll always have a place to stay," Grace yelled to them as Rufus lifted the reins and flicked them on the horse's rumps.

Sara waved at her new friend, then turned and looked ahead at the mountains, looming like giant statues in front of her and swallowed. Talking about doing it had been easy, but now that it was actually happening, the reality was taking hold of her.

A part of Sara was filled with the excitement of the new life they'd chosen, while another part of her was afraid. She wondered if the hardships Lucas spoke about would be too much for her and Rufus to handle. She wondered if the harsh winters would be as bad as Lucas said. And then there would be hostile Indians to deal with, along with the wild animals.

One side of her could understand them not wanting people to come into their part of the world, upsetting the balance of things. People had a way of doing that. She hoped that wouldn't be the case with her and Rufus. She hoped they could make friends with them and learn to co-exist.

During the two weeks it took them to reach the area where his cabin used to be, Lucas tried to teach them as much as he could about living in the mountains, and was surprised at how quickly they adapted.

"You're a born mountain man," Lucas told Rufus after he dropped an elk with one shot.

"We'll see," Rufus told him. "We haven't seen any real hardships, yet. The weather has been tolerable and we haven't been attacked by any mountain lions, bears, wolves or Indians."

"And I hope it stays that way, my friend, but up here, things can change in the blink of an eye."

And just as Lucas predicted, as they slept, the snowflakes began to fall – small at first, but as the night wore on, the flakes got larger and began to pile up.

Rufus felt like a big weight was being pushed down on him and opened his eyes to find the canvas of his and Sara's tent caving in on them.

Off to his right, where Sara's cot sat, he could hear her struggling.

His hands were down along his sides, and he had a difficult time getting them up into position where he could shove, upward. The weight of the snow was more than Rufus could deal with. The tent was caving in on them and there seemed to be nothing he could do about it.

"I'm not gonna let this mountain beat me before I've had a good run at it," he said, forcing himself over on his side and rolling off the cot onto the ground.

Getting his feet under him, he put his shoulders against the sagging canvas and pushed upward with all his strength, and when it began to move upward, Sara rolled out of her bunk and joined him, putting her shoulders against the canvas and pushed them upward.

They were straining hard when they felt the weight begin to lessen. Then came Lucas' voice. "You okay in there?"

"Will be when we get whatever it is that's collapsing our tent, off of it," Rufus replied.

When the tent was once more, free of the weight, Sara opened the front flap and gasped at what she saw. The opening was almost covered up with snow!

Directly, the snow was being shoveled away and Lucas' smiling face appeared. "Like I said, things can change up here in the blink of an eye."

Lucas had a shovel in his hand and they could see where he had shoveled a path to get to their tent. "Get into some warm clothes and come over where I'll have a fire built and the coffee perking," he said, turning and walking back to where he came from.

Lucas had tied a piece of canvas between two trees, sloping it downward in the back, allowing him to keep a small fire burning   something he'd learned to do just after he first came into the mountains. The old mountain man who'd taught him, had said, "You gonna survive up here, boy, you gots ta know how."

When Rufus and Sara came into the tented area and sat down on the logs provided by Lucas, he poured them each a cup of coffee.

"Still got big flakes coming down," Rufus said, taking a sip of the hot coffee.

"How long do these storms last?" Sara asked.

"A few hours, a few days, a few weeks, no way to predict. When they come, you just deal with it, and hopefully you're prepared," Lucas said, shrugging his shoulders.

Rufus looked around at the way Lucas was set up and asked, "Why didn't you show us how to set up our place like you have, here?"

Lucas took a sip of coffee, feeling it's warmth clear down into his stomach. He scratched his new beard and said, "Sometimes, experience is the best teacher. Had I been you, I would have slept inside the wagon. It has a rounded top and high up off the ground. But like I said, a person learns best by experiencing what not to do. Up here, I've seen storms like this come through during the middle of summer."

"So, you never sleep in a tent, even in the summer?" Sara asked.

"That would be true," Lucas said with a grin.

Suddenly, Rufus jumped to his feet. "The horses and mules!"

Lucas waved his hand at Rufus. "Sit back down. Last night, I smelled something in the air and picketed them in amongst some trees with a thick overhang. Checked on them once I saw the two of you were alright. They're doing fine."

During the next three days, the snow storm turned into a howling, freezing, blizzard, and all they could do was to sit around inside the wagon, covered with blankets – the only heat was from the six lanterns they kept burning.

Prior to getting into the wagon, Lucas and Rufus had taken what canvas they had, and made a roof over the area where the horses were kept, while Sara tied blankets over their backs to help keep them warm.

"Still want to be a mountain man?" Lucas asked on the third morning with the wind howling through the trees and shaking the wagon back and forth.

Rufus scratched his growing beard and said, "As the good book says, and this too, shall pass."

Rufus had come up with the idea of covering the underneath part of the wagon with what canvas they had left, making a place where a small fire could be built to make coffee and cook meals, but it had to be put out after each meal so the underside of the wagon wouldn't catch on fire.

When the storm finally passed on, it took another two days before the sun could melt enough snow to make moving on, even tolerable.

"How much farther?" Sara asked as the wagon moved at a slow pace through the snow.

Lucas looked at the sky, then around at the trees and finally said, "Day and a half, maybe two days if the weather holds."

Rufus jerked his head around and asked, "You know something we don't?"

"If you mean, is there another storm coming, I don't think there is, but like I said…"

"I think what he means is, he doesn't know what's up ahead," Sara said, patting Rufus on the arm.

Rufus tightened the reins between his fingers and said, "I knew that."

Unbeknownst to them, two Sioux braves sat on their horses, a short way back in the trees and watched as the horses struggled to pull the wagon up the mountainside.

NINE

When Lucas called a halt, he stared at the charred spot where his cabin used to be and memories came flooding into his mind, along with the hurt. "This is where my cabin used to be, but we won't be stopping here. We still have a few hours to go. And with that, he nudged his horse in the sides.

It was early afternoon when they came up to a rock wall jutting out of the mountainside. Lucas stepped down from his horse and said, "Light a shuck. We're here."

Rufus and Sara looked around and were neither one, impressed. "You want to make camp against the side of a mountain?" Rufus asked, climbing down from his wagon and beginning to unharness his team of mules.

"Wasn't planning to," Lucas responded, ground reining his horse.

"Then why are we stopping?" Sara asked, standing next to the wagon, a curious look on her face.

Lucas looked upward and pointed. "Up there, is a cave big enough for us to stay while I show you around. I think this might be a good place for you to settle down.

There's good protection from the storms, plenty of game and a stream just back in those trees, yonder."

Sara looked up and saw a dark maw in the side of the mountain and decided that it was the front opening of the cave, Lucas was talking about. She could see no ladder or steps going up to the cave and asked, "How do we get up there?"

"There's a place over on the side where a person can climb up, but it's too steep to haul anything heavy on your back. I built a pully, some time back, and if it's still good, I'll climb up and lower the basket down, along with the pull rope and you can fill the basket and we can pull it up."

"What about the animals and the wagon?" Rufus asked. "Won't they be subject to Indians stealing them?"

Lucas rubbed his beard. He never did like growing one. It itched him day and night. "I don't think they have much use for the wagon, although, they might decide to burn it. And as far as the animals go, they would steal them. They truly do like eating mule meat."

"What? No!" Sara said, "We can't let them do that!"

Lucas shook his head. "The lift isn't strong enough to haul the horses or mules up to the cave, but I have an idea that will lessen the chance of Indians stealing them."

Lucas decided to picket the horses just in front of the cave where they could see them and be able to shoot anyone trying to steal them. Also, with Rufus' help, he set out his bear traps and dug holes to plant the spiked sticks in them. And this time, he added cow bells to places in between.

"Whooie, that should stop anybody trying to steal them," Rufus said when they'd finished.

"One way or another, we're bound to hear anybody who shows up, and from the front of the cave, we'll have a clear shot at them," Lucas said with confidence.

By mid-afternoon, the following day, they had everything lifted up into the cave and Sara had started setting up house. She built a fire in the pit that was already there, then toward the back of the cave, she made a place where she and Rufus would sleep, while Lucas put down his groundsheet and bedroll, on the opposite side and closer to the lip of the cave, in case he was needed because of someone down below, like, Indians.

Just before sundown, Lucas and Rufus went into the forest and within half an hour, Lucas brought down a good size buck, deer.

That night, they feasted on deer steaks and canned beans.

-

"Are they planning on living in that cave?" Scar On His Face, asked the brave sitting on his horse, next to him.

Speaks Loudly, tried to speak as softly as he could, but the deep base in his voice carried loud and clear in the evening air. "I do not think so. I have heard of this white man. He lived here with an Arapahoe squaw, many moons ago, and now he has returned with people you cannot see in the dark. I do not know why, but our chief will want to know."

And with that, he reined his horse around and rode back into the trees.

TEN

Most of the tribe lived in teepees, but Bear Killer had his women build a round topped hut, which in his mind, gave him, the chief, more distinction.

Speaks Loudly rode up to the Bear Killer's hut and got down and waited. You did not approach the chief's hut without being invited. Shortly, one of Bear Killer's wives came out and asked what he wanted?

"I have vital news Chief Bear Killer needs to hear," Speaks Loudly told her.

She disappeared back inside the hut and shortly, Speaks Loudly heard the chief's voice. "Come!"

Speaks Loudly pulled the flap aside and entered the hut and stopped. Chief Bear Killer was a huge, bull of a man, standing nearly six feet in height, and weighing over two hundred pounds – towering over the five foot eight, Speaks Loudly, who was one of the tallest braves in the tribe.

Bear Killer was known to have a short temper and every member of the tribe, brave or squaw, feared him, which is just the way Bear Killer liked it. As long as they feared him, he would not be questioned or disobeyed.

Bear Killer stood on the opposite side of the fire in the middle of the hut, his arms folded across his chest. "You say you have important news for me?"

Speaks Loudly took a step closer to the fire and looked up at his chief. "Scar On His Face and I were looking for game over near where the white, mountain man used to live with the Arapahoe squaw."

Bear Killer frowned. He hated long stories. "Get to the point," he said, seeing fear in Speaks Loudly's face. He liked Speaks Loudly and knew him to be a loyal follower, but he was in no mood to listen to a long-winded story, today.

"The white man we knew as, Lucas Penny, is back.," Speaks Loudly said.

Bear Killer ground his teeth together. This could not be! He had killed the squaw and had sat in silence while the white man burned his cabin to the ground, with the squaw inside – then he watched him leave.

"You are sure it is him?" Bear Killer asked, dropping his hands to his side.

"I am sure," Speaks Loudly said. "After he killed several of my friends, his image is burned into my mind."

"And is he alone? Did he bring a squaw with him?" Bear Killer asked.

Speaks Loudly thought for a moment, trying to figure out how he was going to explain the two people he'd seen with Lucas Penny.

"He has brought two people with him, a man and a woman, but they are very strange," Speaks Loudly said.

"What do you mean, strange?" the chief asked, now, very curious.

Speaks Loudly let their image form in his mind and finally said, "They have very peculiar skin. It is black, like meat that has been in the fire too long. It is so black I do not think I could see them in the dark."

What was this? the chief wondered. "Are you sure what you say is true? I know of no people whose skin is black, like burned meat."

Speaks Loudly turned and called out, "Scar On His Face, come inside!"

The flap was drawn back and Scar On His Face came into the hut and stopped short of the two men.

Speaks Loudly looked at his friend and said, "Tell our chief what you saw when we stopped near where the mountain man, Lucas Penny, once lived."

Scar On His Face, swallowed. His fear of their chief showed on his face.

"Speak up! What did you see?" Bear Killer yelled.

"I saw the man we called, Lucas Penny and there were two strange looking people with him – a man and a woman. Both of them had skin so black that you cannot see them at night."

Bear Killer nodded his head, then said, "You may go. I must consider your words."

When they were gone, Bear Killer motioned to the squaw who had just entered his hut. "I need some of the potion to help me think. Prepare it now," he told her.

Within minutes, she returned with a cup filled with a frothy liquid. The chief sat down in front of the fire and took it in his hands. Their shaman used this for his visions, and he would use it to see what he must do about the return of this man called, Lucas Penny, and the two strange people he brought with him.

Bear Killer ordered the squaw to leave and make sure he was not disturbed until he called out to her.

When she left, he sat, staring at the bubbles floating on top of his drink, then slowly, he lifted the cup to his mouth, and drank.

At first, nothing happened, then he felt his body begin to tingle; swirling clouds formed in his mind and he fell over backwards. He was floating on a cloud, looking down at the world. Then, little by little he saw the face of Lucas Penny fill his mind. The man was grinning from ear to ear. He had a knife in one hand, and a scalp in the other. He could see himself lying on the ground with blood seeping from his chest.

Everything turned into a dark cloud with lightning and thunder coming from it, and as it moved closer to him, he saw a black man and a black woman come walking out of it. A light shined about them like a giant halo. They were Gods! The very same gods that protected the mountain man!

Then, everything went black. How long he laid there, he didn't know but when his eyes opened, the fire had burned down to ashes. He stood up and went to the opening of his hut and pushed the flap back. The sky was filled with stars. He looked to the side and saw his squaw, sitting on the ground, her head bent forward, and a soft snoring was coming from her open mouth.

As he went into the surrounding trees to take care of business, he found that he was trembling.

"It was just a dream," he told himself – but he couldn't shake the feeling he was having. Afterall, the shaman swore by his dreams and in many cases, he had been right.

After building the fire back up, again, he sat for a long time, staring at it, trying to make sense of his dream, and in the end, he came to a decision. He had to strike first - kill the two gods, then kill Lucas Penny, before they had a chance to destroy, him.

The thought of killing them brought him alive, again, and he called out for the squaw to come to him.

ELEVEN

Several days had passed and Rufus was of the mind that they wouldn't be attacked by Indians. Over coffee one morning, he told Lucas how he felt.

"To my way of thinking, if we were to be attacked by Indians, they would have done so by now. I'm guessing they're afraid of you."

Lucas, who was curious why they hadn't seen any Indians, said, "Remember what I told you about Indians having patience? Well, this is just like what they'd do. They want you to either, be on edge, always looking over your shoulder and afraid, or think they weren't out there and become lackadaisical, so you won't be expecting their attack."

"You really think they know we're here?" Rufus asked.

"Without a doubt, my friend, without a doubt," Lucas told him.

"So, what are we supposed to do?" Rufus wanted to know.

"That depends," Lucas said, pouring more coffee into his cup.

"On what?" Rufus asked.

"On whether you plan on staying here, or not," Lucas said, blowing on his coffee to cool it down enough to drink.

Rufus took a drink of his coffee. "Sara and I have been talking, and we both like it here. In fact, we think this cave just might be the ideal spot to call our home. We've got nothing to build. It's big enough and you have to admit, it's not easy to attack. Plus, it's easy to heat in the winter and it's cool in the summer."

Lucas nodded his head, and said, "All of what you say, is true, but what about supplies and your stock?"

"We can lift up what things we need on that lift you built. The stock? Well, that's a matter I haven't got figured out, yet. Plus, there's the matter of getting in and out. The climb can be treacherous in bad weather. It's tough even in good weather."

Lucas sipped his coffee as he gave thought to everything Rufus had said, and finally, after sitting his cup near the fire to keep the coffee warm, he stood up and walked over to the edge and looked down, then up to the roof of the cave.

Sara came up next to Rufus and asked, "What's he up to? He sure is doing some hard studying."

"Not sure," Rufus said. "But I think it has something to do with me telling him we're thinking about making this cave, our home."

Sara laid her hand on Rufus' shoulder and asked, "Have you told him about the noises further on down in the cave, yet?"

Rufus looked at Sara and said, "Not yet. I'm still not convinced they're made by anything except the wind."

Sara put her hands on her hips and said, "You can think whatever you want, Rufus Dogwood, but I'm telling you, here and now, the wind doesn't make noises like people talking.

Rufus said nothing, knowing what Sara said was true.

Just then, Lucas came over and sat down, lifted his cup and took a healthy drink, and when he'd finished, he said, "I think I've got you problem of coming and going, solved."

"Well, pray-tell, do enlighten us," Rufus said with a great flare.

"It's simple, actually. We build a manlift. It will be similar to what you're using, now, only bigger and stronger. One person can use it to go up or down."

Rufus grinned and said, "For a white dude, you come up with some good ideas."

Everyone got a good laugh, and by late that very day, they had the new, manlift built and in operation. Getting the heavy logs up into the cave had been the hard part, but once they were up there, the rest was just work. Lucas had drawn up his plan on a piece of paper, which made the work go faster. He had used the extra wagon wheel for the rope to roll on the wheel. Each log was at least twelve inches thick and was strong enough to lift a horse or mule.

Sara was a bit concerned and over supper, she said, "I hope you're not planning on keeping the horses and the mules up here with us. I know that would be the safest thing, but we'd need to bring up food, every day and take away their leavings. Plus, after a while, the stink would be overpowering."

Rufus admitted he'd given that some thought, but had come to the same conclusion she had. "No, we'll have to figure out something to do about the stock."

He looked at Lucas and said, "You seem to be the one with the brains, what do you think we should do?"

Lucas raised his hands, palms forward and said, "Whoa! I'm no smarter than either of you. I just happened to think of the lift thing, first. In time you would have had the same thought. And as far as the stock is concerned, I think we should go down and look around. Maybe one of us will think of something."

The following morning, after breakfast, the three of them went down to the ground and spread out, each trying to find a place to keep the stock without them being easily stolen.

The sun was creeping toward its apex when Lucas and Rufus met at the manlift. Rufus looked around and asked, "Where's Sara?"

Lucas got a concerned look on his face as he stared around, trying to see beyond the trees surrounding their camp, but saw nothing of Sara.

TWELVE

Sara had walked a good distance from the cave in search of a good place to hide the animals, but had found no place suitable and decided to turn back. "This is too far from the cave, anyway," she said to herself.

-

Speaks Loudly had sneaked off, wanting to see again for himself that he had not been seeing things. It would not go well for him if he had been wrong.

Nearly half a mile from the cave, Speaks Loudly pulled his horse to a halt. There in the near distance was one of the gods he had told Bear Killer about. It was the female.

-

Sara was walking back toward the cave, feeling sorry that she hadn't found a suitable place to hide the horses when an Indian brave, riding a paint horse, rode up in front of her and stopped. He was bare from the waist, up, and had a handsome look about him. But he was an Indian and she had heard the stories about what happens to women taken by Indians.

"This is not the time to panic," she whispered to herself.

Without a word, she tried stepping around the horse, but the brave moved with her, continually staring down at her. He had a curious look on his face.

"Please, let me pass," Sara said, as politely as she knew how.

The brave slid down from his horse and approached her slowly. With a certain amount of trepidation, Speaks Loudly reached out and touched her hair, then stepped back. "Are you one of the gods who protect the white man we know as, Lucas Penny?

Sara was taken aback by the good English this Indian spoke. Other than Lucas, everyone else she knew, said Indians were nothing more than filthy, heathens. But this man looked nothing close to being that. His hair was long, and jet black, with feathers braided in it. He looked muscular and healthy. His dark eyes bore into her. The only thing she could see was a man from a different culture than hers. And from all of the trials and tribulations she'd gone though from being born, black, she looked at this man, this Indian, who was studying her and could speak and understand English. Because he was different, the white people didn't like that. Even the Orientals were ridiculed by them.

Did he think because her skin was of a different color than his or the whites, that she might be a god? She almost laughed out loud, but caught herself. Maybe if she went along with him? "Yes, I am one of the Gods who protect Lucas Penny," she said, putting her hands on her hips and staring up at this man who had a certain amount of fear in his eyes. If she yelled, boo, would he turn and run? Seeing his hand on the hilt of his knife changed her mind.

Speaks Loudly stepped back, afraid she might touch him or put some kind of curse on him, and stared down at her. She had a determined look on her face, but something inside him questioned this whole thing. He was known far and wide to be a man who thought things out before rushing in like a foolish child.

He walked around her, looking at her from all angles and his observation told him she was just a mortal, nothing more. Not one to be feared. Of course, that didn't mean he would make any move until he was absolutely, sure. Just because her skin color was different than his, or the white man, didn't make her a god. After all, his skin and the skin of Lucas Penny was different, wasn't it? And just because the mountain man was white, didn't make him a god, either. He had seen forty-six winters and still wasn't convinced the gods his people believed in were as powerful as they were thought to be.

Sara stood, stock, still, not moving as the Indian brave walked around her, appraising her.

Finally, Speaks Loudly stopped directly in front of her and said, "If you are a god, prove yourself. Show me something only a god can do. Make that tree move," he said pointing at a small pine tree, nearby.

"That is not what Gods, do," Sara said. "We are here to serve the ones we are protecting, not doing some magical tricks to make you gasp."

Feeling brave, Speaks Loudly looked down at this woman who said she was a god, and said, "If I tell you I am going to your camp and kill the one you claim to protect, what will you do to me?"

"Nothing," Sara told him. "If you want to challenge Lucas Penny in a fight, so be it. I and my mate will only be there to make sure you don't win. We only step in when the person we are protecting needs our help. And from what I know of Lucas Penny, he will have no trouble overcoming you."

She hoped she sounded convincing enough to stop him from going to the camp.

Although this woman had an air about her, Speaks Loudly still wasn't convinced. She was an attractive woman, even if her skin looked like burned meat.

"What if I say I am going to take you as my woman? What will you do, then?"

Suddenly, Sara was afraid. This man was a well-made man and could overpower her without exerting too much energy. Trying to run away would only convince him she wasn't a god and she had been bluffing. Her best bet was to try to bluff him from trying anything. "If you try to harm me, in any way, the male God who is with me will come and what he will do to you will be worse than having a thousand ants crawl into your ears and up your nose."

"Haw!" Speaks Loudly exclaimed. "I do not believe you!" And with that, he stepped closer and was about to reach out and grab her when he heard a loud voice coming from behind him. "Hey! You! Let her be!"

He whirled around and saw a black man running toward him. His eyes showed a great deal of anger. It was the female God's matc!

"You lay one finger on her and I'll see you in the happy hunting grounds!" the man yelled, raising a pistol in his direction.

It was true! She was a God! She had called for her mate to come to her and he had come.

Not wanting to die, Speaks Loudly ran to his horse and raced away as fast as he could, thanking the gods he was allowed to live to fight another day as bullets tore holes in the leaves of the trees close to him.

"Are you alright?" Rufus asked as he ran up to Sara.

She was trembling and he took her into his arms and held her close to him. "It's going to be all right, he's gone." Rufus whispered in Sara's ear.

Lucas came running into the clearing from a different direction and came to a halt when he saw Sara and Rufus. "I heard gunshots? Was either of you hit?"

Rufus released Sara and turned to Lucas. "No one was hurt. When I got here, there was an Indian brave trying to take Sara, but I shot at him and he jumped on his horse and rode away."

"But you didn't kill him?" Lucas asked.

"No. I wasn't trying to. I just wanted to scare him away. Why? Is that important?" Rufus asked.

"I'm not sure," Lucas said, rubbing his chin. "On one side, he could count his lucky stars he had escaped and that would be it. On the other hand, he could look at it like the gods had protected him, making him invincible."

Rufus nodded his head and said, "In which case he might come back, and try to get her, again, feeling like we cannot harm him."

"That's about it," Lucas said.

Sara stepped up next to Rufus and Lucas and said, "I... well... I... I guess I kind of told him, Rufus and I were gods, here to protect you, Lucas."

"You did what?" Lucas and Rufus said at the same time.

When Sara finished telling what had happened, Lucas said, "I understand. He thought if he could capture a God, it would make him invincible."

"Taking her would make him a very big man in the tribe," Rufus said, looking in the direction the Indian had gone.

"Yes, he would be considered very powerful, and the other braves would follow him if he decided to attack us," Lucas said, gritting his teeth together.

"Let's get back to the cave and make some plans," Lucas told them as he turned back toward the cave.

THIRTEEN

Speaks Loudly rode into the village at top speed and pulled his horse to a dust swirling stop in front of the chief's hut.

He leaped off his horse and went into the chief's hut without announcing himself, leaving a lot of people talking.

"What is this?" Bear Killer said, turning from where he had been talking to his squaw.

"Tell her to leave. I have important information," Speaks Loudly said, louder than he'd wanted to.

Bear Killer bristled up at this insolent brave. "Who are you to come into my hut, unannounced and give me orders?"

Speaks Loudly lowered his head and said, "My apologies, Bear Killer, chief of my people, but what I have to say is of the most importance and is not for woman's ears."

Bear Killer knew of Speaks Loudly's loyalty to the tribe and his ability to sense out the truth of things. He motioned for the squaw to leave, then walked over and sat down in front of his fire, motioning for Speaks Loudly to do the same.

"Now that we are alone, what is it that you want to tell me that is so important?" Bear Killer asked.

Speaks Loudly took a deep breath to try and calm himself down. "I have not only been up close to her, but I have touched her, and I am here now – alive to talk about it."

Bear Killer had no idea what Speaks Loudly was talking about, but decided to see this through. "Who is, she? And what does having touched her have anything to do with whether you are alive or dead?"

Speaks Loudly took a deep breath, blew it out and started over, explaining where he had gone and what had happened, saying, "If she could summon her mate to come and protect her, does that not mean they truly are, gods?"

It was an interesting story. Bear Killer had to admit that. But could it be that Speaks Loudly was too caught up in this, God, thing?

After several moments he looked at Speaks Loudly and said, "That was an interesting story, but could it not be that she is not really a god, as you say, but her calling to her mate, be just a matter of coincidence?"

Speaks Loudly was stunned. He had been there. She had told him she would summon her mate to come and in the blink of an eye, he had arrived. "But… but… Chief Bear Killer, I was there! She said she would contact her mate to come and kill me and he came running out of the forest, yelling at me and shooting his pistol!"

"Yes, that is interesting," Bear Killer told him, but in the back of his mind, he still had reservations. "Leave me. I must think about this."

Speaks Loudly left his chief's hut feeling confused. Why hadn't he been excited at this news? What was there to think about? The woman had told him she was a god and had proved it by calling her mate.

He was temporarily distracted when several of his friends wanted to know where he'd been. With a great bit of flourish, he recounted what had happened and when he finished his tale, they were in awe. As far as they knew, Speaks Loudly was the only brave who had ever actually talked or touched a god. And the fact that he was still alive to talk about it made him a very brave man, and his statis in the tribe was raised to new heights.

He strutted around the camp getting flirtatious looks from the young women.

Bear Killer sat in his hut, allowing Speaks Loudly's story to run through his mind over and over, searching for signs that would show him this woman was not truly a god, but as hard as he tried, he could not find evidence that she was not just as she said she was.

He got up and left the hut, taking his horse and riding off into the woods. He needed to be alone and allow his mind to think clearly.

-

Back, inside the cave, Lucas, Rufus and Sara sat around a fire, drinking coffee – talking about their situation.

Lucas sat his cup down close to the fire and said, "The way I see it is, this cave is a good place to stay. You have plenty of food and water and it's safer from being attacked than down on the ground. And if they are foolish enough to try, you have a good field of fire."

Rufus shook his head and said, "What you say is true, but what about the animals? We can't bring them up here and there is no place down below where they will be safe."

"Yes, that is the only snag in staying here." Lucas responded.

Rufus looked at his friend and asked, "Are you suggesting we leave here and find a new location?"

Lucas thought for a moment, while taking a sip of his coffee, then he said, "I think we have to give that some consideration."

Both Lucas and Rufus watched as Sara stood up and walked toward the back of the cave and stopped.

"What is she doing?" Lucas asked.

Rufus looked at his wife and said, "She says she hears voices coming from somewhere down the tunnel at the back of the cave."

"Voices? What voices? Have you heard them?" Lucas asked. He listened for a moment and then said, "I don't hear any voices, do you?"

Rufus shook his head and said, "No. I keep telling her it is just the wind making sounds, but she says it is definitely voices."

Intrigued by such a notion, Lucas stood up and went to stand next to Sara. He listened and shortly he whispered, "I think I hear something, but I'm not sure what? I guess it could be voices but not in a language I've ever heard."

Sara said nothing, but continued to listen.

After several minutes, Lucas whispered, again, "I think there must be an opening somewhere deep down in the tunnel that the wind passing over the opening is creating sounds that sound like voices. That's all there is to it."

Sara looked up at Lucas and said, "No. What I hear is not wind sounds. It is people talking in a language I've never heard before, but it is people talking and singing."

The way she said it made Lucas have second thoughts. But that is preposterous, he thought. How can there be people living somewhere, deep in this cave. It made no sense and he said so. "I'm sorry, Sara, but that makes no sense. It's just the wind."

And with that, he turned and walked back to where Rufus was waiting by the fire.

"So, you agree, it is just the wind?" Rufus asked.

Lucas nodded his head and said, "Now, we need to get back to discussing what we're going to do, stay here, or go find a new place for you to live?"

FOURTEEN

Bear Killer knew he was getting close to where the mountain man and the two black skin gods who protected him were staying in a cave, high up above the ground. It was a good place to make a camp to keep from being raided, easily, but not a good place from which to protect your horses.

From where he sat, he could not see the white man's horses but knew they had to be nearby. To keep the horses from whinnying at each other and alert the white man to his presence, Bear Killer slipped down from his horse and ground reined him. This would allow him to eat, but not stray too far – something he'd learned from the whites.

Bear Killer moved silently on foot until he was a short distance from the cave. He looked all around the front of the cave, but saw no horses. Taking a guess, he moved to his left and walked a short distance, looking for the horses. But when he'd gone beyond sight of the cave, he stopped and turned around.

"They must be on the other side," he said to himself – which meant he would have to go across the front of the cave where he might be seen. Instead, he walked deeper back into the trees, then made his way to the other side of the cave.

There, just beyond the opening of the cave, Bear Killer saw three horses and a mule. He smiled. Stealing horses was one of the things he was known for. They would make a fine addition to his small herd. "And the mule will make fine eating this winter," he said to himself as he eased up to the animals.

They were pinned inside a rope tied to several trees, which would make it easy for him to cut the rope and steal them. He would just have to be slow, so as not to disturb the horses.

When he crawled inside the rope and stood up, he spoke quietly to the animals who took a look at him, then went back to eating. Using his knife, Bear Killer cut the rope pinning in the horses and used it to make halters and lead ropes.

After putting halters on each of the horses, and leading them to the far side where they could disappear into the trees, he tied them off, then went for the mule.

Now this ole mule was a, long eared, Arkansas white mule who had a particular notion on who he liked and who he didn't and was not bashful about showing his objections. And when Bear Killer got close to him, he took one whiff of the Indian, then began to brey and jump around, kicking up his hind feet.

Bear Killer was startled and not quick enough to get out of the way as one of the mule's hind feet caught him square in the stomach, knocking him a good ten feet or more, backwards.

"Someone is at the horses!" he heard a woman yell. Still trying to breathe right, he got to his feet and ran for the horses.

He leaped on the back of one of them, and lead the other two as he raced into the forest.

Once he got back to his horse, he swapped animals and led his stolen prey back to his camp as fast as he could go.

And when he rode into camp, one of the first people he met was Speaks Loudly. He pulled his horse to a stop, right in front of him and said, "The white man and his two protectors no longer have horses to ride, for I, Bear Killer, the best of the horse thieves, has stolen them!"

Cheers from the others in the camp filled the air.

Speaks Loudly said nothing, but in his mind, he knew stealing horses was a long way from taking the life of the white man when he was protected by the gods.

-

Lucas was the first one into the clearing where the horses had been kept. He stopped and looked around. The rope fence holding them in was gone, along with their three horses. He looked over at the mule, who was enjoying the tall grass and hadn't felt the need to go wandering off.

"Well, at least we still have Hercules," Lucas said as Rufus and Sara came running up.

"What will we do without our horses?" Sara asked.

Lucas looked at her and grinned. "What are you talking about. You don't think I'm going to let him get away with this, do you?"

Sara got a confused look on her face.

As Lucas led them back to the cave, he said, "Look, horse stealing to the Indians is a big game. They pride themselves as being good horse thieves. So, I will go get our horses, plus three of theirs."

"You think you can do that?" Rufus asked.

"Of course," Lucas told him. "Especially since you're coming with me."

"You want me to go into that Indian camp and help steal their horses?" Rufus was filled with at least a hundred objections.

-

After Bear Killer rode into his camp, leading the three horses, his people gathered around him, waiting to hear how he had come about having three new horses.

Sliding down from his horse, he grimaced. Raising his hands in the air, he said, "Once again, I, Bear Killer, Chief of the Sioux, have faced not only the mountain man we know as Lucas Penny, but I have outwitted the two gods he has with him for his protection, and bring back with me, the truth of my success!"

Loud cheers went up, filling the air as Bear Killer reveled in his triumph.

Speaks Loudly stood watching the proceedings and frowned. "Once again, Bear Killer has made himself look good to the people," he said, and spit into the dirt.

That night, there was much celebrating in the Sioux camp. Their chief had proved he was still the bravest of them all. A strong brew made from fermented seeds and fruits, was passed around and with the exception of Speaks Loudly, three of his friends, and the children, everyone was in a drunken stupor.

By the time the moon was well up into the sky, the people of the Sioux camp were feeling the effects of the brew and were fast asleep.

"How did you know they would all be fast asleep?" Rufus asked standing next to Lucas inside the tree line just beyond the Sioux camp.

"Because Indians like to celebrate their victories – especially victories by their chief," Lucas said, studying the layout and the location of the horses. A good size herd stood, grazing the tall grass next to the creek that ran past the camp.

He could see no one guarding the horses and felt they could accomplish their raid without being seen or heard.

Lucas led the way out of the trees and down the small slope leading to the creek, where they waded across. The moon was full and bright and it was easy to spot their horses. He spoke quietly to the first of their horses as he slipped a rope over its head, while Rufus did the same to the other two.

But when it came to the Indian ponies, they shied away from Lucas, not liking his smell. Rufus grinned as he slipped lead ropes over the heads of three of the Indian ponies and they followed him like they'd known him all their lives.

Lucas shook his head and led their three horses into the creek and up the slope and into the trees, with Rufus just a few feet behind.

"Well, that was easier than I thought it would be," Rufus said as he followed Lucas and their horses - walking well away from the Indian camp before mounting up.

"We were being watched," Lucas said over his shoulder.

"What? Who? Where?"

Before swinging up onto his horse, Lucas looked behind them, but saw no one coming.

"There were four of them," Lucas said, touching his heels to the horse's side. They were standing behind one of the teepees, and thought they were hidden - and were to an untrained eye, but I saw them."

"Why… Why, didn't they do something?" Rufus wanted to know. It made no sense to him that they would stand by and allow someone to steal their horses. From what little he knew, horses meant as much to the Indians, as they did to the white men.

Lucas shook his head. "I'm not sure. By all rights, they should have tried to stop us, but they just stood there and watched us walk away with six of their horses. It's hard to understand the ways of an Indian, sometimes. They do just the opposite of what you think they're going to do."

-

Speaks Loudly and his three friends, the only adults not in a drunken stupor, did in fact stand and watch the horses being stolen.

Red Dog had pulled his knife and wanted to go try and stop them, but Speaks Loudly had stopped him. "No. Let them steal the horses. It will bring shame to Bear Killer when he finds out. The people will not let him forget he was taken advantage of so easily."

The three braves nodded their heads, understanding their friend's words.

-

Sara was waiting when Lucas and Rufus came riding in on their horses and leading three new ones.

"So, will he come to get his horses back?" she asked when they were drinking the coffee she'd made.

"I'm guessing he will," Lucas said. "He's been humiliated and wants to save face."

"And just how do you plan on stopping him?" Sara asked.

"By the only way we can, without going to war with them," Lucas said, matter-of-factly. "We move to a new camp – somewhere far away. Hopefully, far enough they won't pursue us. I'm tired of fighting with them or playing their games."

"For sure, I don't like being left afoot, not knowing if I can get 'em back," Rufus said, shaking his head.

"And we just leave the cave to them?" Sara asked.

Lucas refilled his coffee cup and blew on it. "The cave will stay the same as it is. They won't bother it. They think it's haunted. That's one of the reasons I've used it. Oh, they'll fire arrows into it or shoot bullets into it, but they won't live in it. They too, think those wind sounds are voices. They believe they are the voices of the dead trying to lure you deeper into the tunnel so they can steal your soul."

Sara said nothing, but her mind went back to the voices she'd heard and knew in her heart, she was right. She didn't believe they were the voices of the dead, but they were definitely, voices.

The following morning while the Sioux camp was coming slowly alive, Lucas, Rufus and Sara gathered their things and loaded them onto the horses, then rode away to the north.

FIFTEEN

When Bear Killer realized he'd not only lost the three horses he'd stolen, but three of his own, he went crazy, screaming at everyone, blaming them for not keeping watch, while the truth was, he'd been just as drunk as anyone in the tribe. A herd of buffalo could have stampeded through the camp and he would have slept right through it, which Speaks Loudly gladly reminded him of.

"You were so drunk, you passed out and had to be dragged into your hut."

"And what of you? You do not seem to be suffering?" Bear Killer asked.

Speaks Loudly shrugged his shoulders and said, "The funny tasting water does not affect me as bad as it does you."

"Then why did you not do something when the mountain man came and raided our horse herd?" Bear Killer asked, bristling up and puffing out his chest.

Speaks Loudly was not about to admit he'd witnessed the raid and just stood there, letting them steal the horses. Instead, he asked, "Do you not think I may have also been asleep?"

"Were you?" Bear Killer asked, suddenly feeling unsure about Speaks Loudly's loyalty.

Speaks Loudly looked directly at Bear Killer and said, "I saw nothing, nor did I hear anything. If I had, I would have tried to stop him or them." To Speaks Loudly, lying was as easy as telling the truth.

After a frigid bath in the creek and some food in his belly, Bear Killer had Little Doe, his first wife, pack his bags for traveling, then informed the people that he would be going to get his horses back. With a rifle he had stolen, along with a pouch filled with bullets, he mounted his horse with the spots on its rump, and rode away.

A short distance from the cave, Bear Killer pulled his horse to a stop and studied the opening. There was no smoke coming from it as there should have been. Next, he rode around to where the horses had been kept and saw the place was empty. And after circling completely around the area, he decided they had moved on. But where had they gone? Which way would he have gone, had it been him?

He searched for tracks leading away from the cave but found none. "This mountain man, this Lucas Penny, he is very good at hiding his trail," Bear Killer said, "But he is not so good that I won't find it, for I am Bear Killer, and I will not be denied."

For four days, Bear Killer crisscrossed back and forth through the forest until late on the fourth afternoon, he found their tracks! They were slight and only here and there, but they were the tracks of the man he sought... They had to be.

"You did well, white man, but not good enough. You thought I would get tired of chasing a blind trail, and give up. But you do not know the patience of Bear Killer."

That night, sitting in front of a small fire, eating a rabbit he'd shot, Bear Killer tried to make sense of where the white man was headed – and finally came to the conclusion he was headed for the high part of the mountain where the snow never melts, thinking he would not follow him.

It would not do to go back and wait for warmer weather. Warmer weather never came to the high part of the mountain. It was winter all year round. He threw a leg bone into the fire and tore off another piece. "I am not dressed for such weather," he said, feeling the night air getting colder."

He took a drink from the waterskin, then stood up and stared toward the north. To follow the white man, he would need food, warm clothes, and a second horse to carry his supplies. He had all of these things back at his camp, but if he went back, he would be ridiculed for not catching up to the white man before he escaped to the high country.

He was standing – looking toward the north, when he smelled something. It was light, and just a small whiff, but it was something he knew. He smelled, smoke.

After climbing a nearby tree, Bear Killer stood, near the top, looking around, and there, off to the east, a small stream of smoke lifted above the trees and drifted into the air. "Where there is smoke…" he said to himself as he climbed back down onto the ground.

The following morning, Bear Killer rode off to the east, knowing it would be half a day's ride, or more before he found where the smoke was coming from.

The sun had moved beyond its high point when Bear Killer pulled his horse to a stop and sat looking at the small log cabin a short distance ahead. Smoke rose from its chimney. He was high up on the mountain, near where the snow never melted, a place where few men ever came. He wondered why a man would come here so far away from his people? He must be a bad man who has been cast out, Bear Killer thought. "Living this high up, he will have warm robes to stave off the cold," he said to himself.

After leaving his horse ground reined in among the trees, Bear Killer made his way down to the back of the cabin and put his ear against the log, but could hear nothing. He then moved to the side of the building and found a window, but it had a piece of canvas hanging over it, so he could not see inside.

His heart was pounding. What if there were more than one man living here? Or, there could be a woman?

Bear Killer moved away and back into the trees, just far enough so he could see the front of the cabin, but not be seen by whoever might be inside. He studied the problem. He could draw whoever was inside, out into the open, but then he would have to shoot him, which he did not want to do. It was not that he minded shooting white men, but the sound would carry for many miles, and if Lucas Penny was nearby, he might be alerted.

Then another thought came to him. If Lucas Penny heard the sound, and came to investigate, he would be an easy target! But how would he know the mountain man heard the shot and was coming?

After a while, Bear Killer decided Lucas Penny would not bother about a rifle shot. He was on the run and would keep going, no matter what he heard. But what of the two people with him that were supposed to be gods, protecting him?

His mind was in a whirl as he stood there, pondering what to do?

Just then, the door of the cabin swung open and a man stepped into view. He was about the same size as Bear Killer and had long hair and a full beard. He was dressed in whiteman's pants and shirt. He carried no rifle, but a pistol was strapped to his waist.

The man stopped and stretched, then headed for a small barn off to the far side of the cabin.

So occupied with the front of the cabin, Bear Killer had neglected to notice the barn. "It will have animals, inside. Possibly, a horse or mule to carry the things I will need to track down Lucas Penny," he said to himself.

Once the man entered the barn, Bear Killer, quickly made his way around to the side of the barn and then up to the front corner. He took a breath, then he looked around the edge and saw the door was standing open.

Did he dare go inside, where the man might be waiting for him, or so far inside the barn that a surprise attack would be useless.

Even in the frigid air, he could feel himself begin to sweat. He moved over to the opening and peeked inside. Through the crack between the back edge of the door and the barn, he saw him.

The man was at least, twenty feet away, feeding a horse and a donkey. He didn't like donkeys. They were too slow, but it would provide meat for many days. The horse was large and powerful, and would be able to carry his supplies, if he could bring this man, down.

Bear Killer drew his knife and knelt down to wait for the man to come out of the door. He would take him by surprise.

Otis Trimble was a man of thirty-eight and was on the run from his father-in-law. He'd been a farmer down in Kansas and had married Kyle Meyer's daughter, three years back, much to the objection of her father.

Between the lack of rain and the locust the farm never had a chance and he took to drinking. One day, Otis came back to the farm, his snoot filled with moonshine and found a buggy sitting in front of the small house. Inside, he found his wife packing her clothes and other things.

His mother-in-law was taking the bags and boxes out to the buggy and loading them.

In his drunken stupor, Otis tried to stop them, and in the struggle, his mother-in-law was knocked down. Her head hit the stone fireplace and she lay in a pool of blood around her head.

His wife, Lucinda, stood for a moment, in horror, then turned and looked at Otis, rage filling her eyes. "You've killed my mother!" she screamed and ran over and pulled the rifle off the wall rack and pointed it at Otis. "Now, I'm going to kill you!" Lucinda yelled, cocking the hammer on the rifle, then squeezing the trigger.

The bullet tore into Otis' left shoulder and out the backside. Being drunk, and shot, he reacted by pulling his pistol and shooting his wife. She dropped onto the floor – blood seeping from her chest.

When the realization of what he'd done, hit him, Otis dropped to his knees and said, "I'm sorry. I'm so, sorry…"

In his wife's dresser drawer, he found twenty-seven dollars, hidden in a small tin box. He stood there, wondering what to do next. He couldn't go to his father-in-law and explain what happened. How could he explain that while loaded up on moonshine, he'd killed the man's wife and daughter? Kyle Meyer would string him up from the nearest tree and let him hang there until he rotted.

He was a doomed, man.

Tears ran down his face as he sloshed kerosene around the inside of the house. Then, standing in the doorway, he lit a match and tossed it inside. The small, wooden house caught on fire and sent flames into the air.

Knowing his father-in-law would come searching for him, Otis tied his horse to the back of the buggy, then drove away toward Dodge City.

He was only in Dodge City, long enough to sell the buggy and team, then mounted his horse and headed west for the mountains of Colorado, where he hoped to disappear.

Three years ago, he'd come this place, high up on the mountain, far from civilization, hungry and nearly frozen. Falling from his horse, he lay there, waiting to die. "Just as well," he told himself. "It's what I deserve for what I've done."

Giving in to the fact that he was going to die, up here in the mountains, all alone, by starvation and freezing to death, for his sins, Otis closed his eyes and waited for the inevitable to happen.

The next thing he knew, he opened his eyes and saw a man staring down at him. The man grinned and said, "Welcome back, friend. How about some coffee, then maybe, a bit of food?"

He was wrapped in a bearskin and laying close to a blazing fire. He felt warm for the first time in a long time.

The man's name, he learned, was Lucas Penny, who by sheer chance had seen his tracks and followed them. "Not sure why?" Lucas told him. "Curiosity is the best I can come up with."

They became friends and for the next three months, which happened to be the warm months, Lucas helped Otis build a cabin and barn, and did his best to teach Otis, how to survive as a mountain man.

Otis hadn't seen his friend in more than a year, and wondered if he was still alive, as he pitched some dry grass into the bin for the horse and mule, then filled the water trough.

He set the bucket down and stood for a moment. He would like to go down to Denver and just walk around, looking at the people. Maybe stop and talk to some of them, but he couldn't take that chance. "Sure, as I do, I'd run into Kyle and he'd kill me where I stood, no doubt about it."

Otis chuckled to himself. Who was he kidding? He was dead already. Living up here, all by himself with no one to talk to. The only reason he hadn't killed himself was the fact that he was a coward.

Otis walked out of the barn and when he closed the door, he saw an Indian coming at him and felt the knife go deep into his stomach. The pain raced to his brain and he fell to the ground. He looked up at the Indian and his last words were, "Thank you."

Bear Killer dragged the body out into the woods and left it for the animals to eat, then put his horse in the barn with the other animals. Feeling good about himself, Bear Killer went into the log cabin and ate his fill.

After his third cup of white man's coffee, he lay down and went to sleep in front of the fire burning in the fireplace.

That night, he dreamed of riding in front of a large army of braves, raiding, and taking many scalps.

SIXTEEN

Bear Killer woke up, feeling well rested for the first time in quite a while. The white man's bed had been comfortable to sleep in. He would have a leisurely breakfast, then go back to searching for Lucas Penny.

Little did Bear Killer know that today, things would not be going the way he planned.

As the sun climbed above the tree tops, Lucas rode out onto a wide ledge and looked toward the north and saw the snow-covered mountain top. A mile or so ahead, Lucas pointed to the smoke rising above the tree tops and said, "That's where we're headed. Friend of mine, by the name of Otis Trimble, lives there."

Sara looked around and asked, "Does he have a woman to care for him, or does he live up there, all alone?" She couldn't imagine anyone living up here, so far away from anyone to talk to. At least she would have, Rufus and Lucas when he visited.

"Last I heard, he lives up here all by his lonesome," Lucas said. "Some men prefer it that way. Although, I haven't seen him in more than a year, so I guess we'll find out when we get there."

A little over an hour later, Lucas pulled his horse to a halt, just at the edge of the clearing in front of the cabin, and called out, "Hello, the cabin. It's your ole friend, Lucas Penny!"

Lucas watched and waited for a response to his calling out, but none came, which made Lucas curious. It wasn't like him not to respond, unless he was injured, sick or dead. He could count out that last one. If Otis was dead, there wouldn't be smoke coming from his chimney. Being injured or sick was a strong possibility. He thought he'd taught him not to go off hunting and leave a fire burning.

Once again, in case the man hadn't heard his first call, Lucas called out, "Hello, Otis. It's me, Lucas Penny!"

Still, there was no answer.

Inside, Bear Killer was close to panicking. He'd slept late and was just eating some of the man's food, and wasn't prepared for anyone! Especially Lucas Penny!

He looked around and found out the cabin had only the front door. There was a window in the bedroom, but nowhere else. There was, however, port holes here and there, where a person could put the barrel of his rifle through and shoot at whoever or whatever was in front of the cabin.

Otis went to the door and opened it just wide enough to peek out and what he saw, made his heart begin to race and his breathing, labored. He had not heard wrong, it was the mountain man, Lucas Penny!

"How did he know I am here?" he asked himself as he eased the door closed. "It was the two Gods! It had to be, them. That was the only way the man would know where he was.

Lucas, being a man who noticed things other men might overlook, saw the door open, just a slight crack – just enough for someone to see who was outside.

When the door closed, Lucas pulled his horse back inside the tree-line and turned to Sara and Rufus.

"What's wrong?" Rufus asked, seeing something in Lucas' eyes.

"I'm not sure," Lucas said. "There's someone inside, but it's not my friend, Otis."

Rufus looked around and said, "Are you sure? It's not like there are close neighbors who might come calling."

"If Otis was all right, he would have come out to greet us, but the door opened just a crack so someone could peek out," Lucas said checking the loads in his pistol and rifle.

"So, what do we do?" Rufus asked, checking his own weapons.

Lucas thought for a moment, then said, "I'm going to keep an eye on the door, while you circle around and go check the barn. If someone tries to come out of the cabin, I'll be able to tell if it's Otis, or not. Once you're inside the barn, there should be a large, roan, mare, and a donkey in there. If there's more than that, come back and let me know."

Lucas watched as Rufus slipped off into the woods and smiled. Whether he realized it or not, Rufus was becoming a mountain man.

Inside the cabin, Bear Killer was trying to figure a way to get out of the cabin and get to his horse. If it was just him and the mountain man, he might have a chance, but the man had two, Gods, protecting him! How could he fight against that? He could not, he decided. His best chance was to get to the barn and get away to fight another time and place.

Lucas found a place to throw a fur robe on the ground, then laid down on it in a prone position, with his rifle at his shoulder, ready to fire if the wrong person came out of the cabin. He had no idea who might be in the cabin, and Bear Killer was the last person he would have thought of.

Sara stood a little further back inside the trees, holding their horses so they wouldn't bolt if shooting started.

She looked into the woods where her husband had gone and saw how he was changing from a city man, to a man who was meant to live up here, where survival was a daily event. She admitted, only to herself, that she missed the hustle and bustle of the city – of the talking with other women, of going to the store to buy what she needed, instead of shooting it, or making it. But Rufus was her man and she would go wherever he went.

Rufus eased up next to the barn and listened for sounds from inside, and the only sounds he heard was an occasional snort, or stamping of a hoof, coming from a horse.

Before approaching the door, he took a look in the direction of the cabin and saw no activity. In four, quick, strides, he was inside and stepping behind a stack of hay, where he waited and watched. When he decided he was the only human inside the barn, he stepped out and walked down in front of the stalls. The big, roan, mare was there, and the donkey was there. But also, there was another horse. One who didn't look like a white man's horse. This one had feathers braided into its mane and tail. This was an Indian pony.

Rufus was about to go back and tell Lucas what he'd found when a thought exploded in his head. "If the Indian, somehow got out of the cabin and into the barn, he might escape. But if there were no horses to ride, he would be trapped.

Using great care, Rufus tied the two horses and donkey in tandem and led them out of the barn and into the woods.

Bear Killer opened the door just wide enough to fit the rifle barrel through it and looked for someone to shoot at and spotted the woman leading the horses deeper into the woods.

He hesitated just long enough for her to disappear from sight. He sighed and said, "Maybe it is not a good thing to shoot a god. Of course, he still wasn't sure they were gods. If he got another chance, he might try.

A bullet ratcheted off the door and passed just above his head. Bear Killer pulled in the rifle barrel and slammed the door just as a second bullet slammed into it.

Lucas hadn't tried to kill whoever was inside in case it was Otis and maybe out of his head from sickness or something. That could happen to a man up here.

When the door slammed shut, Lucas called out, again. "Otis! It's me, Lucas Penny. If that's you in there, open the door! I'm here to help you, my friend!"

There was no answer and Lucas was in a quandary about what to do. If his friend was dead, he was bound to see to his killer. If the killer was the one inside, he could burn him out, but they needed the protection of the cabin, so that wouldn't work. Another storm was coming and would be here by morning so he had to figure something out, soon.

Bear Killer had only one thing on his mind at this point, and that was to somehow get to the barn and get away. He would pick another time and place to do battle with the mountain man and his gods. Standing next to the fireplace was a double bitted axe and Bear Killer got an idea. He would chop a hole in the back wall of the cabin, which would allow him to get to the barn, unseen.

As they say, "The best laid plans…"

The wall was much thicker than he'd thought and the wood was aged and hard. After a few minutes with very little result, he gave up and, in his anger, threw the axe into the fireplace.

He was running out of time and he knew it. The man had called out again, a short while ago, but nothing since. Bear Killer went to the door and cracked it open just enough to look outside, and when he saw a rifle barrel come from behind a tree, he slammed the door closed. Trying to leave the cabin by the doorway, was useless.

Lucas contemplated rushing the cabin, but knew that was a useless idea. If the door was barred, which he knew it would be, it would take a big, Arkansas mule to kick it in. And he wasn't about to burn it down. Rufus had already said something about liking it here, if Otis had passed on.

During their evening meal, they discussed the problem and Rufus told them, "I think we should wait him out. How long can he go without water? Whenever what water he has is gone, he'll have to come out, and we'll be here waiting on him."

"An Indian can last a long time without food or water," Lucas reminded him.

"We have any other place to be?" Rufus queried.

"We'll take turns watching the place," Lucas finally agreed.

It was close to midnight when Bear Killer decided to make his escape. The inside of the cabin was cold and completely dark when he opened the bedroom window and looked out. The clouds were covering the moon and even with his keen eyesight, he couldn't see the mountain man's fire and concluded; if he couldn't see them, they couldn't see him.

Like a snake, Bear Killer climbed over the windowsill and slithered down to the ground, then belly crawled to the back of the cabin.

At the back of the cabin, Bear Killer stood up and took a deep breath, waiting, listening for any sound, but the only sound he heard was the rustling of the wind blowing through the trees.

Quietly, he made his way into the trees, then to the back of the barn, where there was a small door he could use to gain access to the barn.

Once inside Bear Killer stopped and let his eyes accustom themselves to the total darkness. He had always prided himself on his night vision. He could go where most other men could not.

When he felt he could see well enough, he was about to walk further into the barn, but stopped and listened. Something was bothering him, and that something was the lack of the horses or donkey making noises. The barn was as quiet as a graveyard.

The hair on the back of his neck began to rise. He drew his knife and held it at the ready, as he moved from stall to stall.

By the time he reached the front of the barn, Bear Killer was in a fit of anger. The white man had beaten him, again!

"Do not let anger overpower your thinking, for it will cause you to make many mistakes," he told himself.

Once more at the back of the barn, Bear Killer eased himself out into the forest and was circling around to come up on the white man's camp from the far side when he happened upon the horses grazing quietly. And there, among them, was his own horse.

"Eyeee," he whispered, believing the gods were now, looking favorably down on him for a change.

He eased in among the horses and made his way up to the side of his horse and rubbed his neck, saying in a whispered tone, "Are you rested and ready to run?"

In response, the horse shook it's head up and down.

He was about to mount it and run away, as fast as he could. But before he did, Bear Killer had another thought. Why not take all the horses. How favorable to his people would he look if he came back with a whole string of horses. Would he not be considered the best horse stealer in the tribe? Even Speaks Loudly would have to admit Bear Killer was the best of the horse thieves in the entire tribe.

He'd just finished tying all the horses together in a string, when he heard noises off to his left. He quickly tied the horses to a branch and went to investigate.

On the far side of the camp, Bear Killer saw the outline of a man standing next to a tree, staring at the cabin.

Taking his knife from its sheath, he made his way up to the man and stopped short. It was one of the gods, the male god! His first impulse was to kill him, but another thought came to his mind. What if he captured the god and took him back with him as his prisoner? Would he not be considered the greatest chief of them all? To capture a god and make him suffer in front of the people;

140

his power would never again be questioned. Not even by Speaks Loudly.

With a quietness most white men cannot come close to; Bear Killer made his way up behind the god and stuck his knife to his throat. "Do not make a sound or I will kill you," he whispered – then moved him quietly, back to where the horses were tied.

Somewhere around four in the morning, Sara went to take her turn at watching the cabin, but when she got there, Rufus was nowhere to be found.

Trying to be as quiet as she could, Sara called out in a loud, whisper, "Rufus. Rufus, where are you?"

When there was no answer, she went to where Lucas was sleeping and called out to him from a safe distance because she knew touching him to wake him up might get a fist in her face. He was very touchy about how he was awakened. "Lucas. Lucas, it is I, Sara. Rufus is missing."

Lucas opened his eyes and sat up, asking, "Did I hear you right? Did you say, Rufus is missing?"

"I went to take my turn at watching the cabin, but when I got there, he was not there. I called out to him, but got no response. Where do you suppose he's gotten off to?"

Lucas stood up, put on his hat, then strapped on his gun belt and finally, pulled on his boots.

Sara followed him as he trotted to the spot where Rufus should have been, and looked around. He pointed at the ground. "See that?"

Sara looked at the ground but only saw where the ground was messed up. "What am I looking for?" she asked.

Lucas pointed and said, "Two men scuffled, and one of them was wearing moccasins."

"Oh, no!" Sara said. "Do you think?" She wouldn't allow herself to consider the thought that Rufus might have been killed by the Indian.

Lucas laid his hand on her shoulder and said, "No. I don't think he's dead. I think the Indian, somehow got out of the cabin without being seen, and when he found no horses in the barn, he came looking for them. I also believe when he found the horses, he also found Rufus and took him prisoner."

Sara gave a sigh, and said, "At least he's alive, and that's a good thing."

"Maybe, not," Lucas said, shaking his head. "The Sioux have ways of torturing a man until he begs them to kill him. Which is the purpose of torturing him, to see how strong he can be. The Sioux respect bravery and hate cowards."

"So," Sara said, "To die with honor, a man must suffer long and painfully?"

Lucas nodded his head. "That's about the size of it."

Sara knew Rufus to have a stubborn streak and would not give in easily, and ventured another question. "How long does a man of honor last before he dies?"

"Depends on the man," Lucas said. "With Rufus, it might take long enough for us to catch up to them and try to break him free. Knew of a man that lasted a month."

From where the horses had been pasturing, it didn't take Lucas long to find their tracks, leading back down the mountain. "Looks like they're moving at a fast pace. He must want to get back to his people as fast as he can."

Lucas and Sara were afoot, carrying only what they absolutely needed. They had to stop, several times because Sara was having a hard time keeping up the pace. "You go on," she told him, but Lucas would not leave her, alone – not in the woods where there were man-eating animals who would find her a tasty feast.

"I doubt he'll start torturing him until he gets back to his camp. There, he'll be able to show his power over Rufus, which will make him a big man."

Sara, somehow, forced herself to go on at the leg-numbing pace. She would not allow her husband to suffer pain and possibly die, just because she was too weak to go on.

Bear Killer rode up next to a small stream and slid down from his horse, then, after dumping the man on the ground, he allowed the horses to drink.

While the horses were drinking, Bear Killer dragged Rufus over and sat him up against a tree, then went about making his camp.

On their way down the mountain, Bear Killer had killed a rabbit with a rock, along with a female wild turkey, also with a rock. He was afraid to fire a gun because the sound travels a long way in the mountains, and he had no doubt, the white man, Lucas Penny, would be coming for his god.

Over a fire, he roasted the rabbit and the hen turkey. He would eat well, tonight.

Rufus found himself tied to a tree, not far from the fire and the smell of meat, cooking. His mouth was also, dry and he was in need of a drink.

Eyeing the Indian squatted next to the fire, who was, contently chewing on a piece of rabbit, Rufus asked, "Is it customary for an Indian to let his prisoner die of thirst and hunger?"

Bear Killer turned his head and glared at the man who was supposed to be a god. "I did not think gods needed food or water."

Rufus thought for a moment, then said, "I do not know about all gods, but this one does."

Bear Killer did not want to take his prisoner back to his camp, half-starved. No. He wanted the man strong so he could show his power over him.

He filled the man's waterskin with fresh water and took it to him, holding it to his lips while he drank.

Next, Bear Killer cut off one of the hen's legs and held it up to Rufus' mouth. "Eat."

Rufus looked at Bear Killer and said, "It would be much easier if you untied my hands."

Bear Killer smiled and said, "The gods must think Bear Killer is a fool. Who would release the hands of a god so he could do his magic? No. You will eat from my hand or you will not eat."

Rufus would like to have his hands free to fight against this arrogant Indian who thought he'd captured a god, but he wasn't easily fooled. He'd have to come up with something else.

He ate the bird-leg, chewing every mouthful, slowly, savoring the meat and its juices.

Rufus watched the Indian closely, trying to second guess his every move, in case he was able to free himself from his bonds.

When the Indian curled up next to the fire, Rufus found he too, was having a hard time staying awake, and drifted off.

Rufus found himself being shaken awake and the Indian who called himself, Bear Killer, standing over him. He put the waterskin to his lips and said, "Drink."

Rufus looked at Bear Killer and said, "I need to go into the woods and do my business, first."

Bear Killer glared at him and said, "No. Now, drink and eat, or you get nothing. The choice is yours."

As Rufus drank, he felt the warm liquid run down his leg. He glared at Bear Killer, vowing to himself that when he got the chance, he would kill this man."

Lucas knew Sara was not going to be able to keep up the pace he was setting, but he also knew he couldn't leave her behind.

Over that night's meal of beans and dried beef, Lucas said, "Come morning, you will be very stiff and sore. I have some salve that might help. Rub it on everywhere it hurts. In another day, your pains with begin to go away, some, as you become accustomed to the steady walking."

"Does it ever go completely, away?" Sara asked, rubbing the salve on her legs...

"No. But it becomes tolerable," he told her with a grin.

The following morning it was all she could do to stand upright and every step she took, made her joints, scream with pain, but she gritted her teeth and went on. The thought of what Rufus might be suffering became her motivation.

At noontime when Lucas called a halt, Sara dropped to the ground, then got back up and began pacing around.

"Leg cramps?" Lucas asked, tossing her the tin can with the salve in it.

They were close to a stream and Lucas suggested she wade out into the cold water. "It might help, before you add more salve. I plan on going back upstream a-ways, and submerge my whole body."

Sara nodded her head and said, "That sounds like a good idea."

The water was cold and it made her shiver, but it also took away some of the pain. While she was wading around in the clear, cold, mountain stream, she could see fish swimming around and stopped. She lowered her hands into the water and waited. Within a few minutes she had two, nice size fish, flopping around on the shore.

Pleased with herself, she got out of the water, rubbed some of the salve on her sore places, then got dressed.

She was cleaning the fish when Lucas came walking into the camp with two more fish. "Great minds think alike," he said as he set his alrcady, cleaned fish down next to the fire. "They'll go good with the beans," he said with a broad smile.

With their bellies full of fish and beans, they moved on and Sara decided she didn't feel as sore as she had when they stopped for their noontime break.

By late afternoon, when Lucas called it a day, Sara's pains were down to just aches. "Where did you get that salve? It works wonders."

Lucas got a strange look in his eyes as his memory went back to the day Crying Dove first rubbed the salve onto his sore muscles. He still missed her, and for a while had climbed into the bottle to help him get over his misery. But that was in the past. He could now think of her with fond memories. "My Indian wife made it."

"You were married?" Sara asked. "To an Indian woman?"

"Well, there wasn't actually a ceremony or anything like that. She was Arapahoe and I rescued her from the Sioux brave who kidnapped her. And after a time, we just took to one another and had what you might call, an understanding. She was my woman and I was her man."

Sara could see the sadness in Lucas' eyes and decided not to pry any further, but he continued on.

"We had a good life together, Crying Dove and me. But the Sioux didn't cotton to us being together and they finally caught her alone one day and... killed her. Of course, I did what I felt I needed to do, then I left the mountains and crawled into a bottle for a long time."

"I'm so sorry," Sara told him, wishing she hadn't brought up sad memories.

"Thank you. It's okay to talk about it now. I have some wonderful memories of our time together. And I guess that's all a person can ask for."

Sara wondered how she would feel if the Sioux killed Rufus? Angry, for sure. Sad, yes, definitely. She loved him dearly and until right now, she'd never given much thought to one of them dying. She looked at Lucas and asked, "Do you think we'll be able to find Rufus in time?"

Lucas thought for a moment and finally said, "Afoot, like we are, and don't take this wrong, but by myself, I could come close to making as many miles a day as they will riding the horses. But - and this is not your fault, but you still need to get your body used to trotting for long periods of time. And that will come, but it will take practice. Between getting your body in condition and your lungs used to the thinner air, it takes a lot of doing."

Lucas closed his eyes for a moment, then continued. "Will we catch up to them in time to save him? I honestly don't know. But what I do know, is, we're damn well going to try. As I said before, I don't believe he'll kill Rufus until he's shown his power over him, in front of the people of his tribe. Will we be able to get there before Rufus has had to undergo a good deal of punishment? I doubt it. But he's tough and won't go down, easy."

Once again, Sara wanted to tell Lucas to go on without her, but she knew it would do no good. He wouldn't leave her out here, all alone. As she rubbed salve on her calf, she said, "Then I'll just have to toughen up, faster. You set the pace and I'll do my best to keep up.

SEVENTEEN

Rufus stood, tied to a tree. His head was hanging down. His naked body was covered with welts and blood was leaking from the cuts.

Bear Killer stood back and smiled. What was left of the switch he'd cut was worn down to just a stick. The branch had been nearly five feet long and now there was no more than two feet left.

They still had two more days of travel before they would reach his camp and he did not want this man who claimed to be a god, to be seen by his people as strong. He wanted them to see him, defeated. And so, he had stripped the man, naked, cut the switch and thrashed him until he was covered from head to foot, with bloody welts. That would show his people that he was more powerful than this God!

It took some doing to get Rufus onto the back of his horse. The horse kept shying away because he didn't like the smell of blood.

Bear Killer finally had to hobble the horse, front and back legs, to get him to stand still long enough to load Rufus, belly down across the horse's back.

When the task was finally done, Bear Killer was breathing hard and was feeling the hardship of his years. With a smile on his face, he walked over and mounted his horse. Even at his advanced years, he would be going back with the pride of a conquering warrior, and his people would honor him for what he'd done.

In two more sunrises, he would be looked at, once more as, Bear Killer, a powerful chief.

Anxious to get back, he pushed the horses a little faster – but the donkey refused to be made to run. Bear Killer gave considerable consideration to killing the donkey, but did not. He wanted to give the donkey to his people as a present, like he would any other animal he brought to them as meat for them to eat. He knew donkey meat would bring him great statis – so, he allowed the donkey to set a slower pace. An extra day would not change the outcome of his returning as a conquering warrior.

154

That night, Bear Killer once again, tied Rufus to a tree and fed him just enough to keep him alive. As he sat next to the fire, sipping the white man's coffee he'd taken from the cabin, he remembered something else he'd brought along – planning to share it with his people. Salt.

He rummaged through the pack and found the sack filled with salt. There was also one filled with sugar, but it was the salt he wanted to find.

Taking a little in the palm of his hand, he walked over to where Rufus stood with his head hanging down. "This will wake you up," Bear Killer said as he rubbed the salt into the cuts on Rufus' body.

Unable to hold the scream back, Rufus came wide awake and screamed into the night.

Sara and Lucas had just laid down for the night when the scream echoed its way across the night wind.

Both Sara and Lucas sat up.

Sara said, with pain in her voice, "That is Rufus! We must be close to them. Get up we have to go find him!"

Lucas sighed and said, "As much as I'd like to, you have to understand, they are still a long way ahead of us. Sound travels far up here in the high country."

Sara began to cry. Her man was being tortured by some heathen Indian and there wasn't anything she could do about it.

Lucas felt sorry for Sara, but there was nothing he could do about it except maybe say a few words to give her hope. "At least we know we're gaining on them and if you're up to it, we'll leave at first light. Maybe we can catch up with them before they get back to his tribe."

"I'll be ready," Sara said, gritting her teeth. Pain or no pain, she would do whatever it took to free Rufus.

The following morning, just after the sun cleared the horizon, both Lucas and Bear Killer set off at almost the same time. The only difference was, Lucas and Sara were setting a strong pace, trotting for a while, then walking to ease their muscles and get their breathing under control, then back to trotting - eating up the miles. With her desire to find Rufus, Sara no longer felt the pain in her joints and muscles. Rescuing Rufus was her number one goal.

Bear Killer, on the other hand was slowed down by the donkey's unwillingness to be made to go any faster than a walk. Plus, from time to time he would stop and crop grass.

Bear Killer cursed the donkey and vowed to see him roasting over an open fire. Even so, he was making better time than Lucas and Sara because, Sara in her eagerness to keep up with Lucas, stepped into a divot in the ground and twisted her ankle.

Lucas wrapped it as tight as he dared, and even though she vowed to keep going, it was at a slower pace.

That night Lucas made camp next to a small stream where Sara could soak her ankle and sore muscles in the cold water. And again, they heard the agonizing screams of Rufus as salt was rubbed into his wounds.

Sara had never been accused of being a violent woman, but at this moment, she wanted to tear the skin off the Indian's body, one piece at a time and stick a burning piece of coal against the raw meat and listen to him scream.

By morning, the swelling had gone down considerably and with it wrapped tightly, she was able to move faster than yesterday. She was still not able to run, or even trot, but sheer determination allowed her to set a brisk pace.

Crying Dove had been a strong woman and Lucas could see the same determination in Sara's eyes. She would do to ride the river with.

The sun was well up in the sky when Bear Killer rode into his camp with his hostage and stopped in the middle of the camp, next to the fire. He sat on his horse and waited for his people to gather around him, and when he finally spoke, it was the voice of a warrior, home after a victorious battle.

"I have had a long and difficult journey. I have faced the gods that protect the mountain man we know as Lucas Penny. And I have returned, victorious!"

There were cheers from everyone but Speaks Loudly, who stood off to one side, wondering how this old man had been able to go against the gods and win? But it was true. Did he not have one of them tied across the back of a horse? He did not like to admit it, but Bear Killer truly was a mighty warrior. But he would hear his story before he made his decision to challenge the old chief, or not.

Bear Killer slipped off his horse and untied Rufus and pulled his mutilated body off the horse and dumping him on the ground.

Bear Killer strutted around the limp body of the black man and said, "I bring to you, one of the gods who claim to protect the mountain man to show you, my power! He has faced Bear Killer and lost!"

There was much cheering and Bear Killer felt his success. He would remain chief.

He glanced over the heads of the people and saw Speaks Loudly standing in front of his teepee, with his arms folded across his chest, and said to himself, "Before this day is over, Speaks Loudly will admit he is not strong enough to challenge me for the right to be the chief of this tribe. No man here is as strong a leader or warrior, as me."

Within minutes, Rufus' naked body was strung up, spread eagle, between two poles, and the women were gathered around him, poking him with sharp sticks and the children were throwing rocks at him. One rock hit Rufus squarely in the left eye, causing it to swell completely, closed. Another hit him in the mouth and knocked out two teeth. The final blow was one to his head that sent him into a darkness he never recovered from. His body was already undernourished, and dehydrated from not enough water and the sharp sticks that had punctured holes in his body, with several of them finding vital organs. The rock to the head had knocked him unconscious so he didn't feel the pain of his organs shutting down and bleeding to death, internally.

When morning came and Bear Killer found that Rufus was dead, he was sad. Not because the man was dead, but because he had not seen him suffer more before he left this world.

Even though the man hadn't lasted through a long and torturous ordeal, he still used the man's death to his advantage. Standing in front of Rufus' dead body, Bear Killer raised his arms in the air and proclaimed, "Even the gods cannot stand up against the Sioux! We are the mightiest people of all the tribes. With Bear Killer as their leader, no one can stand against us!"

Loud cheers rose into the air, as one of Bear Killer's followers, Crow Killer, stepped up next to his chief and raised his hands in the air, and when they had quieted down, he said, "Hail to Bear Killer, the mightiest chief of them all, whose name should be changed to, God Slayer!"

And so it was, that day, Bear Killer was endowed with his new name, God Slayer, and took his place as the undisputed chief of the tribe. He sat in front of his hut and received presents from his people as their way of showing their loyalty. Everyone that is, except Speaks Loudly.

When the last of the presents had been given, Speaks Loudly approached his chief and said, "I bring no presents for I am not yet convinced you battled the god face to face and came away victorious. Someday, I will find out the true story of how you came to be in possession of such a prize and I will show you up for the deceiver you are."

And with that, Speaks Loudly turned and walked away, leaving God Slayer, shaken. It was true, he had not faced the god in battle but had sneaked up on him and put a knife to his throat. But didn't his ability to sneak up on a god and take him prisoner mean something?

That night when Little Deer came to comfort him, he found he was not up to it. He was still shaken by Speaks Loudly's words and ordered her, away. That night, he lay awake for a long time, trying to find a way of getting rid of Speaks Loudly without anyone knowing it had been him.

When the sun brought lightness to the new day, God Slayer sat in front of his fire, eating his breakfast, feeling the fatigue from his lack of sleep.

"What is troubling you, my chief," Little Deer asked, knowing something was wrong. He had never sent her away, before.

Trying to mask his real thoughts, God Slayer said, "It is nothing. I am still tired from my long battle. I will be myself again in a few days. Now, I need to be alone to think."

Little Deer bowed her head and backed away, leaving the hut, still unconvinced he had told her the truth. She had been his woman long enough to know when he was lying.

As she walked down to the creek to get fresh water, she noticed Speaks Loudly, staring at his chief's hut. He had a smug look on his face and his arms folded across his chest.

She knew Speaks Loudly wanted to be the chief of their tribe and her instincts told her, he was the reason God Slayer was not himself. She would keep an eye on Speaks Loudly to see what he was up to.

EIGHTEEN

Three days later, Lucas and Sara creeped up to where they could see the Sioux camp from hiding.

Lucas pulled out his long glasses and held them to his eyes. Things looked peaceful enough, which made him wonder why things were so quiet. Bringing in a prisoner was a big deal and there would be much celebrating, but the people were milling around as they normally did.

He was moving the glasses around the camp when he brought them to a halt. There, hanging between two poles, was the body of Rufus. He could see the bugs climbing over his body, feasting on the bloody cuts. They were too late. Rufus was dead.

"What do you see? Can you see Rufus? Is he okay?" Sara asked.

Lucas lowered the glasses and took a deep breath, then shook his head, no. "I'm sorry, but we're too late."

Sara gave a gasp and bit hard down on her lower lip hard enough to draw blood. She reached out for the binoculars and said, "I want to see for myself."

Lucas drew them away from her outstretched hand and said, "I don't think you should."

Sara knew what she would see would be bad, but no matter. She wanted to see for herself. "Please, I need to see for myself," she said, still holding out her hand.

Reluctantly, Lucas handed the long glasses to her.

Sara put the glasses to her eyes and looked at the camp and when she found Rufus' dead body hanging between the two poles, she almost screamed her pain and anger.

Instead, she lowered the binoculars and handed them to Lucas, saying, "They will pay for what they've done."

She then stood up and walked back in among the trees.

Lucas watched her go and decided to give her time to grieve as he turned his attention back to the Sioux camp, looking for a way to find the brave who killed Rufus.

It wasn't long before an Indian came out of the only hut in the camp and seemed to be highly regarded. "That's him," Lucas whispered to himself. "That's who kidnapped Rufus and tortured him before bringing him back to this camp. He was more than likely half dead by the time he got him back. The squaws would have done the rest."

Lucas gave thought to putting his rifle to his shoulder and killing the man, but if he did, they would be after him in a heartbeat, and there was Sara to consider. Plus, how far could they get without any horses.

He watched as a woman exited the hut with a chief's headdress and handed it to the brave everyone was patting on the back.

"So that's who it is. Bear Killer, the chief," Lucas said. He'd heard of him but they had never come face to face, but that was about to change if Lucas had anything to say about it.

He eased back far enough so he wouldn't be seen if he stood up and when he'd gone only a short distance, he saw Sara standing in a small clearing, and she was staring at him with a look that made him shiver.

"Were you able to see the one who killed Rufus?" she asked.

"I did. It was Chief Bear Killer, their leader," Lucas said, matter-of-factly. "I'm not quite sure how I can get in and get Rufus' body and kill Bear Killer, but I'm working on it."

"Never mind about Rufus," Sara said. "Neither of us is big on having words said over us or being buried for that matter. What's done is done. It's the man who killed him, that I want, and it isn't up to you. It will be me who kills him."

Lucas stood there and stared at Sara. This was not the woman he'd known. She had suddenly become hardened - a woman on a mission. She interrupted his thoughts by saying, "Can we steal a couple of horses so we can get away from here?"

"I suppose so, but…" was as far as Lucas got when she interrupted him. "We need to get far away from here. They'll still be here when I decide to come back."

"When you decide to come back?" Lucas asked, not sure where this was going and not sure he wanted to know.

"You'll be teaching me how to shoot both a pistol and rifle, how to use a knife, and fight like a man. Once I've learned those things, I'll come back for this, Bear Killer."

"Now Sara," Lucas said. But before he could say more, she said, "I want to see him so I will know him when I come back."

They went back to their hiding place and Lucas gave her the binoculars and described Bear Killer.

She looked through the long glasses for only a short time then lowered them and asked, "How do we go about getting our horses back?"

Late that night a rain storm came roaring through. It was like fate had come to help them. The sky was filled with dark, rolling clouds. The rain came down in torrents and lightning struck the ground, making deafening noises, causing the horses to jump and kick up their heels. It was an ideal time to do what Lucas had in mind.

The brave guarding the horses had ducked under a tree to get as much protection as he could and was more interested in staying dry than he was in protecting the horses.

During one of the lightning flashes, Lucas had watched the young brave run for cover and knew exactly what he was going to do.

Between the sound of the downpour rain, the wind, the lightning and the horses jumping around and nickering, there wasn't much use in trying to walk softly as Lucas came up on the young brave from behind.

Lucas decided not to kill him, but instead, render him useless by knocking him on the head with the butt of his pistol.

Sara followed Lucas into the frightened horses and helped tie a string of six horses together.

Before leaving, Lucas left on foot and shortly returned with the body of Rufus, and tied him over the back of one of the horses. Sara said nothing, but in her heart, she was glad Lucas had gone after him. Together, they drove the other horses away into the forest, following them for several miles before pulling away and heading north.

When the storm finally passed, Swift Antelope came to take his turn guarding the horses and found his friend, unconscious and lying face down in the mud. He was not dead but he had a large lump on the top of his head. And all their horses were gone!

Swift Antelope raced back into the camp, shouting for people to get up. And as he ran up in front of the chief's hut, God Slayer came out of his hut, asking, "What is all the shouting about?"

When Swift Antelope told him what happened, God Slayer ground his teeth together and asked, "Which direction did they go?"

"I have not taken the time to check. I came to tell you, first," Swift Antelope said, hoping he'd done the right thing.

"What you have done is good, but I need to know which direction they went," God Slayer told the young brave.

"I will get Speaks Loudly. Next to you, he is the best tracker in the tribe," Swift Antelope was quick to say.

When Speaks Loudly got to the place where the horses were kept, God Slayer was already there, walking around, trying to tell which direction the thieves had gone even though he was sure he knew who the thief was. It had to be the mountain man, Lucas Penny, because the body of the black man, was also, gone.

Speaks Loudly could see the tracks of the horses, all heading east. He scouted around in all directions before coming back to stand in front of God Slayer. "Whoever he was, he was smart. He rode with the herd as he drove them to the east, making his tracks mix with the other horses."

"Somewhere, he will pull away and that is the place we must find, although I am sure I know who did this and which direction he will go," God Slayer said, as he turned and walked back to his hut and went inside, calling over his shoulder, "Have the braves meet at our fire. I will be there, shortly.

Within minutes, six braves set off on foot to find and bring back their horses. Because of the storm, the muddy tracks were easy to follow.

God Slayer promised he knew who had done this and where he could find him and as soon as the horses were back, they would go after him and not come back until they had his hair on a pole.

NINETEEN

Lucas did not go back to the cabin, nor did he go back to the cave. Instead, he took them to a hidden valley he'd seen several years ago. He'd always meant to go back but until now, things had always come up.

The small valley was six days ride from the Sioux camp and Lucas knew they could not wait that long before burying Rufus' body.

Rufus was buried inside a small grove of trees. And when Lucas was finished, there was no sign that anyone was buried there. Along with looking just like the rest of the forest, there was no marker, for if the Indians found it, they would more than likely dig him up and leave the remains for the animals of the forest to feed on.

Before leaving, Sara stood for a full fifteen minutes, alone, with Rufus, saying her last goodbye. Before leaving she said, "Do not worry, I know who did this to you and I promise to see him suffer before he dies."

And with that, she turned and walked to where Lucas was waiting with the horses.

For the next five days Lucas led them to the northeast – neither of them having much to say. At night, they would find a place close to water. Lucas would see to their camp and hobble the horses. Sara would prepare their meal, then wash the pots and pans.

Lucas had questions he wanted to ask Sara, but stayed quiet, allowing her to grieve in her own way. He figured she would talk when she was ready.

In the early afternoon of the sixth day, Lucas and Sara pulled their horse to a halt on top of a hill that overlooked a small, but beautiful valley. It was barely three quarters of a mile, across it, in any direction. There were scattered trees. The grass stood tall and green – and waved back and forth in the gentle breeze. A small creek made its way through one side, and standing there, drinking their fill were a dozen deer.

Lucas spoke for the first time that day. "As I recall, deer, elk, moose and other animals come here to feed and drink. And that creek is loaded with fish. A person would have to be a real tenderfoot to not be able to survive here."

"It's beautiful," Sara said, gazing across the valley, feeling safe and comfortable for the first time since their stealing the horses. "Yes, I believe this will be an ideal place for what I need to do."

"And what is that?" Lucas asked.

"I want to know how to hunt and trap game. I want to know all the survival skills a person needs to know to live up here," she said, pointing toward the high country. "I want to know how to shoot with both a pistol and a rifle. I want to know how to fight with a knife, and my fists. I want to become a mountain woman."

Lucas stared at her for a long while, then asked, "Are you sure about this? There are plenty of men who can't do what you're asking. The hardships are many and your chances of survival are small."

"Oh, I will survive," Sara said. "I made a promise to Rufus and I mean to keep it."

They rode down into the valley with Lucas shaking his head. She had plenty of grit – at least, right now, but he would wait and see how she fared out when the going got rough.

The first thing Lucas decided to do was build a place for them to live. And as it turned out, it was larger than he would have built for himself. This one had two bedrooms, a kitchen, a living room with a rock fireplace, built with rocks from the creek. The water for use in the kitchen and for bathing, came from them digging a trench from upstream down to the cabin into a cistern sort of hole. Gravity would bring the water down to the house where it emptied into a rock lined hole next to the back door of the cabin. Lucas also built a small fireplace in the kitchen for Sara to cook on.

Sara worked alongside Lucas, just like a man. She chopped down trees, trimmed them and helped set them in place. She made a sled like affair to haul rocks up from the creek for the fireplaces. And when Lucas cut pieces of lumber for making the table and chairs and bed frames, Sara tied the pieces together with long strips of bark that she wove into ropes.

After a month of hard labor, not only did they have a comfortable cabin to live in, they also had a barn where the animals could be housed during the cold months that were just around the corner, so to speak.

Sara spent many hours on her knees, cutting grass for Lucas to haul up to the barn to store for the coming winter months.

She also helped Lucas dig a trench that fed from the creek to the barn that fed into a long water trough that could be shut off by a piece of wood that would slide down into the water trough, stopping the flow of water, to keep it from flooding the barn.

Two days after completing the cabin and barn, Lucas sat quietly down close to the creek, but a short distance away and waited. He'd been there for less than two hours when a large moose came down to the creek to drink.

Sara heard the boom of the rifle and knew they would have meat to eat and possibly a skin to cover one of the beds.

Lucas was more than pleased at the way Sara pitched in and never shied away from anything he asked her to do. He'd decided, sometime back that if she wanted to learn the way of the mountain man, then he would do it the same as if she were a man. It was the only way to make her strong enough to endure all she needed to learn.

During the winter months, Sara learned to fight like a man. They would make their way out to the barn, and get to it. At first, Lucas had a hard time punching a woman, but she told him not to hold back. He was surprised at how quickly she learned and just how hard she could hit.

Next, came the knife fighting and he found her to be surprisingly quick to learn and fast with her movements. He had several small scars to prove it.

But what she excelled at was her quick draw and accuracy with a pistol. She was better than he was, and he told her so.

She proved herself on several occasions by drawing and shooting a rabbit or squirrel on the run.

They each built snow shoes and went off into the forest where he taught Sara how to survive in the cold, by digging a small cave in a snow bank and building a fire to survive the bone chilling nights – along with the other things she needed to know. And it wasn't long before she would leave on her own and be gone for two or three days, and each time she came back with a deer, an elk, or antelope.

By the time spring finally arrived, Lucas felt he'd taught her all he knew about being a mountain man, and baked her a cake to celebrate.

"Today, I am proud to say, you have become a true, mountain woman."

She raised her cup of coffee because they had no alcohol, and said, "I owe it all to you, Lucas Penny, and I thank you. Rufus would be proud."

A week later, she packed up what she thought she would need and told Lucas she might be gone for some time. "However long it takes to do what needs to be done," she said.

"And that is?" Lucas queried.

"You know why I'm leaving. You've known since the first day you started my training. I'm going to avenge Rufus' death," she said, placing her hands on her hips. "And don't try to stop me. My mind is set."

"Wouldn't think of it," Lucas told her. "He was my friend and I'll be going along with you."

He stayed their leaving until the next morning, so he could pack, lock down the cabin and turn out the stock left behind so they could survive until they got back. This was to be her home. He would be moving on once their work was done.

TWENTY

As they rode away, Lucas marveled at the change in her. Sara Dogwood was no longer the same person he'd met so long ago. And she no longer dressed like a female. She wore men's buckskin clothes and from a distance, if you didn't know better, you would mistake her for a man.

She could fight, shoot and hunt better than most of the men he knew. About the only thing she didn't do was, chew tobacco and drink whiskey.

During their six-day trip, her mind was like a sponge, learning everything she could about Indians and their ways of thinking. Lucas knew he didn't know everything about all the different tribes, but enough for her to be on firm ground when dealing with them.

If they survived this trip, she would return to the cabin a much stronger woman – a woman who would stand a good chance of surviving because the Indians would be afraid of her. After all, they thought she was a god.

The only other woman he'd heard of living up here, alone, was Crazy Cora, a widow woman whose husband

and three children had been killed by the Kiawah. The only reason she hadn't been killed was during the raid, she had run around the yard, swinging a butcher knife, shouting scriptures at them. They thought she was crazy, which may have been true. Indians mostly shy away from people they thought were crazy. The gods would not look favorable on them for killing a crazy person.

As far as he knew, she still lived in the same cabin, high up in the Rocky Mountains and tended her garden and the graves of her husband and children. And from time to time, a brave would leave a deer or elk for her, so she wouldn't put a curse on them.

They made good time and late afternoon of the fifth day, they found themselves, back in the close proximity of where the Sioux camp was located. At least they hoped it would still be there. Indians were known to move their camps to follow their needs.

After a night of tossing and turning, his mind going in all directions, Lucas and Sara rode up to as close as they could, then, after securing their horses, went on foot the next half a mile and belly crawled up the slope to where they could look down on where the camp should be.

Lucas gave a slight sigh when he saw it was still there. He looked at Sara and indicated with his head for them to move back.

When they got back to the horses, Sara asked, "What's the plan?"

Lucas took a deep breath and said, "Mount up. We'll move back a mile or so where we can make camp and talk about it."

The camp was well hidden inside a small stand of trees where the smoke from their fire would dissipate in the tree limbs and not be noticed by anyone.

Over coffee, Lucas said, "I think we need to look at this from several angles. One, we know Bear Killer lives in the hut, not one of the teepees, so that makes it easier to find him, but not necessarily easier to get to."

Lucas blew on the hot coffee, then took a sip. It was strong, just the way he liked it. "At first, I thought we might sneak in during the night while he was asleep and do what needs to be done, quietly, then fade away into the night. But after seeing where his hut is situated in the camp, I'm not so sure that's our best option."

"What if we create a distraction? You could do something to draw them away, while I sneak in and avenge Rufus. And when I get in the clear, I could send you a signal," Sara said.

Lucas thought for a moment, then said, "That sounds like a good plan, except for one thing."

"What thing is that?" Sara asked.

"If there is a distraction," Lucas said, "what is to keep Bear Killer from going with the rest of them to see what's going on?"

Sara shook her head and said, "Good point."

For the next hour or so, they sat in silence before Sara asked, "Do you think I could get into the camp and inside his hut without being seen?"

"Maybe," Lucas told her. "If everybody's asleep and there are no guards. What do you have in mind?"

The small sliver of the moon was well past its zenith and mostly hidden by clouds when Sara crawled up next to the edge of the Sioux camp and waited. Lucas had argued that he should be the one taking the chance on sneaking into the camp and doing away with Bear Killer to avenge Rufus' death, but she had stood strong. Rufus was her husband and it was up to her to see the man who did it, was punished. And in the end, she had won the argument. After all, wasn't that why she'd learned all she could from Lucas, and wasn't she now, as able as any man?

She counted to three hundred, slowly, giving Lucas, time to get in place. Easing up onto her hands and knees, she surveyed the area and saw no one. Her luck was holding out, they were all asleep.

Very slowly, Sara stood up. There were half a dozen teepees to get past before she could get inside the chief's hut. She was wearing moccasins which would allow her to make her way to the hut without making any sound. When she decided Lucas should be in place, she left the shadows of the trees and walked at a steady pace toward the hut.

Lucas, was indeed, in place and about to fire his pistol, stampeding their horse herd as a distraction. The horses would draw the Indians away from the camp, while Sara entered the chief's hut and did what she felt she needed to do. He just hoped she had the courage to go through with it. After all, as far as he knew, she'd never killed a man with a knife, before. It was one thing to shoot a person from a distance, but killing a man with a knife, was done up close where they stood the chance of defending themselves.

Just as he raised his pistol in the air, he heard half a dozen dogs begin to bark. "Damn," he said to himself. He'd forgotten that every Indian camp he'd ever been into, had dogs running around freely, ready to yelp their heads off if a stranger entered the camp.

He fired three shots into the air to stampede the horses and as they jumped and ran off, making a lot of noise, Lucas ran back into the trees, and circled around to where he could make his way to the chief's hut. And as he got close, he heard a great deal of commotion going on, inside.

Ten feet from the hut, several dogs ran up to him, barking their heads off. One of them tried to reach in and bite him, but Lucas kicked him in the head and he backed away.

Lucas entered the hut with his gun in his hand and found Sara, wrestling with not only Bear Killer, but a squaw as well.

The squaw turned and saw Lucas and rushed at him with a knife.

Lucas grabbed her wrist and tried to twist the knife from her grasp, but she held it tightly and began to kick him, and tried to bite his hand.

Lucas looked over her shoulder in time to see Sara drive her knife into Bear Killer's stomach, and watched him drop to the ground.

Just then, a brave came running into the hut.

Lucas shoved the squaw toward Sara, then turned to face the brave.

In a panic, with her adrenalin running at high speed, she made quick work of the squaw and ran to help Lucas, who yelled at her, "Go! Get out of here!"

"I'm not leaving without you!" she yelled as she drove her knife into the brave's side.

Lucas slung the brave aside and the two of them raced for the door and ran outside, only to be confronted by at least twenty braves, who were pointing rifles and arrows at them.

Speaks Loudly, entered the hut, then immediately returned. He walked up to Lucas and Sara, who were now being held by the braves, and said, "God Slayer is dead. I, Speaks Loudly, am next in line, and proclaim that I, am now, Chief of the Sioux!"

While not all of the braves cheered, the ones who followed Speaks Loudly, did.

The ceremony that would assure his place as chief, would come in a few days, but for now, no one opposed his stepping into the role.

As Sara and Lucas were being taken to the poles where they would be tied until it was decided what to do with them, Sara remembered what Lucas had told her about them being afraid of crazy people.

Suddenly, she stopped, jerking away from the brave holding her arm, and began singing and dancing around, pushing herself provocatively at the male braves, who jumped back – their eyes wide with shock and fear. The female god had gone crazy and might be calling to other gods to come and strike them down.

Sara knew she couldn't take the time to try and rescue Lucas, too, or they might figure out what she was up to, so, wasting no time, she left the camp, singing and calling out to the heavens.

Once she was inside the trees, she began to run, astounded they had let her leave.

When she got to the horses, she mounted hers, and rode away, leading the other one.

She wasn't sure how far she'd run the horses, but when she stopped and climbed down, she could see they were lathered and panting hard.

"I'm sorry," she said, leading them to the small, nearby, stream. She unsaddled them, then led them out into the water to help cool them down, then let them roll in the grass.

From what Lucas had told her, she didn't think the Indians would follow her. She figured they were just glad to be rid of her.

That night, over a small fire, she drank coffee and prayed they would not kill Lucas before she could return and try to get him away from them. She was suddenly overwhelmed by what she'd done and now Lucas may die because of her need to avenge her husband's death.

TWENTY-ONE

Speaks Loudly strutted up to where the white man, hung between two poles. He had been stripped of all his clothes, and switched until he was covered with bloody welts.

"I see your protective god has gone crazy and left you to us. You will suffer long and painful before you die for your crimes against the Sioux, Lucas Penny."

When Lucas raised his head and stared at him, Speaks Loudly grinned and said, "Oh yes, I, Speaks Loudly, knows who you are and I am not afraid of you. As the new chief, I will show them I am not afraid of you, or your gods. I will become known as the chief who killed the mountain man, Lucas Penny and drove away the god who was sent to protect him."

Speaks Loudly turned to face the women and children standing behind him, and said, "You may switch him and throw rocks at his body, but only to bring him pain. I want this man to stay alive until I say it is time to send him to the great beyond."

And with that, Speaks Loudly strode away, making plans for the ceremony that would officially make him chief.

Lucas steeled himself against the rock throwing and the switching, and no longer felt the pain. Somewhere, deep inside his brain, he knew Sara had not gone crazy. She had only been pretending so she could get away and figure out a plan to come back for him. His lips spread open making a small grin as remembered the transformation she'd gone through. Speaks Loudly was about to come face to face with a woman on a mission. A woman, more fearful than any he'd ever come up against.

TWENTY-TWO

Sara walked along the bank of the creek. She'd just finished eating two, large trout she'd caught in the stream and was feeling bad that she had not yet come up with a plan to rescue Lucas. Her last plan had backfired because of forgetting about the dogs. This time, there could be no mistakes. She stopped and looked at the stars, saying, "Please, God, don't let him suffer too much until I can find a way to get him out of there."

The following morning as she rode away from the stream, she saw a man, dressed in mountain man buckskins, riding a mule, and leading a second one, coming in her direction. She pulled her horses to a halt and waited.

The man rode up and stopped in front of her and sat, staring at her, before he finally gave a nod of his head. He'd never seen a black person before. "Is you human? And if so, is you a man or a woman?"

Sara took a good look at him and what she saw was a grizzled man in what she guessed to be his forties. His hair and beard were long, and his beard had bugs crawling around in it, eating the bits and pieces of food that had been trapped there. He was short, about her size and the skin on his face looked the color of leather. He had definitely been in these mountains for some time.

"I'm human and I'm a mountain woman, mean as a female bear protecting her cubs and short tempered as an Irishman whose liquor has been taken away from him, and I can out shoot, out fight and out cuss any man in this part of the country," she said, watching the man's eyes go wide.

"I do declare, I think I believe you," the man said. He lifted his hat and said, "They call me Dancin' Jack cause I surely do like to cut a rug. Why I've been know ta…"

He was cut short by Sara riding up next to him and putting her hand over his mouth.

"I'm not interested in sitting here, jawing. I've got me a job to do, and just maybe I might let you help."

Dancin' Jack eyed her suspiciously, and said, "Job? I'm not much inta doin' physical labor, ma'am."

"How do you feel about Indians?" She asked.

Dancin' Jack swallowed, not liking the question. "I don't have nuthin' again 'em as long as they don't bother me. Fact is, that's why I'm up here. I trade with 'em."

"What have you got in those packs?" Sara asked, pointing at the second mule.

"Gee-bobs, mostly. Trinkets. Shiny things. Some knives, matches ta light fires with. Things like that. Why do you ask?"

"What do you know about the Sioux?" Sara queried.

The man grinned and said, "Ole Bear Killer and me is on friendly terms. I usually give him something a little extra when I go there to trade. Last time I was here, I gave him a nice skinning knife. He was real pleased about that. This year, I brought him a derby hat."

Sara gave a sigh and said, "He won't be needing it."

"Why's that?" Dancin' Jack asked.

"Cause he'd dead. I killed him," Sara replied.

"You what?" Dancin' Jack exclaimed. "Who took his place? Not Speaks Loudly, I hope."

"That's exactly who the new chief is," Sara said, looking directly into Dancin' Jack's eyes and seeing the confusion that was suddenly there. "You have a problem with that?"

"Not exactly," Dancin' Jack said, rubbing his hand over his beard. "He ain't as social as Bear Killer was. He tolerates me cause he likes the knives and things like that, that I bring."

Sara suddenly got an idea and asked, "Do you think you can hold their attention for a few minutes. I mean, the whole tribe."

"Always do. Fact is, I usually spend most of the day barterin' with 'em. They like ta barter, ya know."

He eyed her and asked, "Why you askin' me that? You up to somethin'?"

"You happen to know a man called, Lucas Penny?"

"I do. He's ah good man," Dancin' Jack said. "Why do ya ask?"

"Because they're holding him hostage and it's because of me he's probably stretched out between two poles and being tortured."

"Because of you, you say?" Dancin' Jack asked, now curious and wanting to know more.

When Sara finished telling him the story, Dancin'
Jack shook his head and said, "We'd best quit wastin'
time. Like I said, Lucas is ah good man, and if I know
anything about Speaks Loudly, he'll take days, or even
weeks, makin' Lucas suffer before he allows him ta die.
What do you want me ta do?"

The following morning, shortly after they'd finished
their morning meal, the people of the Sioux tribe heard
bells jingling and a trumpet blowing as Dancin' Jack
came riding into their camp. "Hello to my Sioux
friends," he called out in their language.

He was suddenly surrounded by every man, woman,
and child of the tribe. He climbed down and took a sack
from one of the packs and began handing out pieces of
stick candy. And in just a couple of minutes, he had them
eating out of his hand, so to speak.

While Dancin' Jack was entertaining the Sioux tribe,
Sara sneaked up behind Lucas and whispered, "Are you
awake?"

Lucas whispered back, "What are you doing here?
Get out of here before they see you!"

"Oh, I do plan on leaving as quickly as I can, but when I do, you'll be coming with me!"

Lucas felt the hide straps being cut and he fell to the ground.

Instantly, Sara was helping him to his feet and together they slipped, quietly away to where Sara had their horses tied, in among the trees.

"Climb aboard and let's get out of here. I've got clothes for you, back at the camp," she told him as she helped him up on his horse. He was weak and still in a lot of pain.

Back at her camp, Lucas washed in the stream and then, Sara treated Lucas' wounds as best she could.

"I'm afraid you'll have to eat on the run. They'll notice you're missing and come looking for you," Sara said, helping him onto his horse and handing him a piece of meat.

"Was that Dancin' Jack, I heard?" Lucas asked as they rode away.

"It was," Sara told him. "I'll explain, later," she said as she slapped her heels against the side of her horse.

An hour later, they rode between two, large boulders and up a short incline into a wide space among the rocks.

There, squatting next to a small fire, Dancin' Jack was sipping from a tin cup. He looked up and said, "Glad ta see ya made it. Drop down and have some coffee."

While Sara was putting together a small pot of stew, Lucas heard the whole story.

"And when I figured Sara had time to get you down and outta there, I opened my pack and dumped all my gee-haws on the ground, tellin' them I'd be back ta get my hides, later, and lit a shuck for here. I didn't want ta be no-wheres around when they found out you is gone.

Lucas stuck out his hand and said his thanks, then, over stew, he said, "If you'll come with me, I've got me a small gold mine, or cave to be more precise. I can see that you're repaid for your gee-haws, and then some."

Dancin' Jack thought for a moment, then said, "I think I'll take you up on your offer. Don't think I'll be welcome back to the Sioux camp.

Six days later, they rode into the yard where Sara's cabin stood, and when they went inside, Dancin' Jack said, "I declare. This here is the fanciest cabin I've ever seen."

Lucas and Jack spent the next two days helping round up the horses and putting up more hay for the coming cold weather.

On the third morning, before leaving, Lucas stood before Sara and asked, "Are you sure you're going to be all right?"

She smiled and took his hand, saying, "I'll be just fine. And, if you ever happen to be in the neighborhood, drop by for a decent meal."

"That goes for you, too, Dancin' Jack," Sara called out as he came walking up, leading his two mules.

Dancin' Jack walked over and said, "I'll be right proud ta come visitin'. And maybe next time, we can have some music and kickin' up our heels."

"I'd like that," Sara said as she stepped up and gave him a hug and a kiss on the cheek.

Dancin' Jack's face turned the color of a ripe turnip and he said, "Come next spring, you keep an eye out cause ole Jack will be ridin' in."

Sara stood for a long time, staring in the direction her two friends had gone. And when she turned to go to the cabin, off to her left, she saw a young wolf, sitting just at the edge of the trees, staring at her.

At first, she was startled, but when he just sat there, she walked into the cabin, then returned shortly with a piece of meat in her hand. About half way to the trees, she stopped; then tossed the meat as close to him as she could.

The young wolf sat there for a long time, staring at Sara and the meat. Finally, he walked slowly down to where the meat lay on the ground – took it in his jaws and walked back to the trees.

Sara smiled and went back to her cabin. She had things to do.

The young wolf lay on his stomach and chewed on the meat, keeping his eyes on the front door of the cabin.

Five days later, Lucas and Dancin' Jack rode into the clearing in front of the cave, not knowing that Speaks Loudly and twenty braves were less than a half a day away, riding in their direction. Speaks Loudly had only one thing on his mind – to see Lucas and Dancin' Jack, skinned alive, and staked out over an ant hill.

THE END

ALSO BY JARED McVAY

Other works by Jared McVay

Jared McVay is an award-winning author who writes, Westerns: A western series: Historical Fiction: Action/Adventure: YA: Children's books: screenplays: teleplays: Short stories, and also does storytelling.

NOVELS:

Western: Clay Brentwood Series- 10 Books:

Historical Fiction: The Legend of Joe, Willy & Red – award winner

Historical Fiction: Silent Runner, Guardian Warrior

Western: Hacker's Raid – award winner

Historical Fiction: Legend of Jubal Courtney

Action/Contemporary - Not on My Mountain – double award winner

JUVENILE FICTION

Brody O'Shea – 3 Books

SCREENPLAYS

The Hobos

Jared & the Warden

Talltree

TELEVISION PILOT SCRIPTS

McClusky [6 episodes] - Drama/Comedy

ACT Acute Care Transport - Drama/Comedy

Melinda: Award winning short story

MEET THE AUTHOR

Jared McVay lives in Oregon where he writes his books, does storytelling, book signings, speaking engagements, and gets in a little fishing from time to time. Before becoming a novelist, Jared was a professional actor – stage, film and television, and a ghostwriter for screenplays.

As a young man he worked as a cowboy, a rodeo clown, a lumberjack, barker for a carnival and a truck driver. During the 1950's he rode the rails as a hobo and during the 80's, a blue water sailor. He spent his military time in the US Navy Sea Bees, where he learned his electrical trade as a power lineman, then spent ten years as a lineman for Kansas Gas & Electric. But it was his love of entertaining people that led him into acting and writing.

Jared has five children, eleven grandchildren, fifteen great grandchildren and four great, great grandchildren.

THANK YOU
FOR READING!

If you enjoyed this book, we would appreciate your customer review on your book seller's website or on Goodreads.

Also, we would like for you to know that you can find more great books like this one at www.CreativeTexts.com